CHANGE UP

CHANGE UP

DEREK JETER

with Paul Mantell

JETER CHILDREN'S

SIMON & SCHUSTER BOOKS FOR YOUNG READERS

New York London Toronto Sydney New Delhi

SIMON & SCHUSTER BOOKS FOR YOUNG READERS
An imprint of Simon & Schuster Children's Publishing Division
1230 Avenue of the Americas, New York, New York 10020
This book is a work of fiction. Any references to historical events, real people, or
real places are used fictitiously. Other names, characters, places, and events are
products of the author's imagination, and any resemblance to actual events or
places or persons, living or dead, is entirely coincidental.
Text copyright © 2016 by Jeter Publishing, Inc.
Jacket illustration copyright © 2016 by Tim O'Brien
All rights reserved, including the right of reproduction
in whole or in part in any form.
SIMON & SCHUSTER BOOKS FOR YOUNG READERS
is a trademark of Simon & Schuster, Inc.
For information about special discounts for bulk purchases, please contact Simon &
Schuster Special Sales at 1-866-506-1949 or business@simonandschuster.com.
The Simon & Schuster Speakers Bureau can bring authors to your live event. For
more information or to book an event, contact the Simon & Schuster Speakers
Bureau at 1-866-248-3049 or visit our website at www.simonspeakers.com.
Book design by Krista Vossen
The text for this book was set in Centennial.
Manufactured in the United States of America
0316 FFG
First Edition
2 4 6 8 10 9 7 5 3 1
CIP data for this book is available from the Library of Congress.
ISBN 978-1-4814-6445-1
ISBN 978-1-4814-6447-5 (eBook)

*To my father and all of the coaches
who dedicate their time to helping
others grow as athletes and individuals
—D. J.*

A Note About the Text

The rules of Little League followed in this book are the rules of the present day. There are six innings in each game. Every player on a Little League baseball team must play at least two innings of every game in the field and have at least one at bat. In any given contest, there is a limit on the number of pitches a pitcher can throw, in accordance with age. Pitchers who are eight years old are allowed a maximum of fifty pitches in a game, pitchers who are nine or ten years old are allowed seventy-five pitches per game, and pitchers who are eleven or twelve years old are allowed eighty-five pitches.

Dear Reader,

Change Up is a book based on some of my experiences growing up and playing baseball. While I worked hard on the field, I was encouraged by my parents to do my best off the field as well, in my schoolwork and in supporting my team, teammates, and family.

I have tried to keep basic principles in mind as I work to achieve my dreams. This book is based on the third of those principles, Deal with Growing Pains. That is the theme of this book. I hope you enjoy it.

Derek Jeter

DEREK JETER'S 10 LIFE LESSONS

1. Set Your Goals High (*The Contract*)

2. Think Before You Act (*Hit & Miss*)

3. **Deal with Growing Pains** (*Change Up*)

4. Find the Right Role Models

5. The World Isn't Always Fair

6. Don't Be Afraid to Fail

7. Have a Strong Supporting Cast

8. Be Serious but Have Fun

9. Be a Leader, Follow the Leader

10. Life Is a Daily Challenge

CONTRACT FOR DEREK JETER

1. Family Comes First. Attend our nightly dinner.
2. Be a Role Model for Sharlee. (She looks to you to model good behavior.)
3. Do Your Schoolwork and Maintain Good Grades (As or Bs).
4. Bedtime. Lights out at nine p.m. on school nights.
5. Do Your Chores. Take out the garbage, clean your room on weekends, and help with the dishes.
6. Respect Others. Be a good friend, classmate, and teammate. Listen to your teachers, coaches, and other adults.
7. Respect Yourself. Take good care of your body and your mind. Avoid alcohol and drugs. Surround yourself with positive friends with strong values.
8. Work Hard. You owe it to yourself and those around you to give your all. Do your best in everything that you do.
9. Think Before You Act.

Failure to comply will result in the loss of playing sports and hanging out with friends. Extra-special rewards include attending a Major League Baseball game, choosing a location for dinner, and selecting another event of your choice.

CONTENTS

Chapter One

CURVEBALL

I can't believe it. My dream is finally coming true!

Derek Jeter sat in the back of his family's old station wagon, thinking those words, not saying them out loud, as he watched his dad get behind the wheel and fish out his car keys.

Instead Derek said, "Thanks for doing this, Dad. I know how busy you are, but I'm reeeeally happy you're coaching our team." *Finally,* he wanted to add, but stopped himself.

"I'm as excited as you are, Derek," Charles Jeter said, smiling as he glanced at his son in the rearview mirror. "It's the first time I've ever coached a team."

"Really?" Derek was shocked, although he probably shouldn't have been. Mr. Jeter had been a college player until he'd injured his knee, but since then had been working, studying for advanced degrees, and raising a family. Still, Mr. Jeter had been Derek's unofficial coach practically since Derek was in diapers. It seemed weird that his dad had never coached a baseball team until now.

"Wow! We get to be your first team," Derek said proudly.

"I just hope you'll be as happy about it when the season's over as you are right now. You might not be, if we wind up in last place."

Was he joking? Derek wondered. Probably. His dad always kept a straight face, so it was sometimes hard to tell what was a joke and what wasn't. But *would* Derek still be happy if their team wound up in last place?

That was not going to happen, he reassured himself. Never in a million years. His dad was the best coach in the world! Or at least the best Derek could ever imagine. Who else could have taught him so well, and cared so much, and believed in him so totally? His dad knew everything there was to know about baseball, Derek was sure of that.

Suddenly he remembered something. "Hey, Dad, don't forget to pick up Vijay at his house!"

Vijay had been Derek's best friend since the Patel family had arrived in Kalamazoo and moved into Mount Royal Townhouses, just a stone's throw from the Jeter family's townhouse in the same development. The Patels were from India, and they were the first Indian-American family Derek or any of the other local kids had known.

Derek had been Vijay's first friend in town, and they'd been best friends ever since. And now they were on the same team—for the third year in a row!

Derek's *other* best friend, Dave Hennum, was on the team too. In fact, the entire universe seemed to be aligning to produce the one thing Derek had never experienced in his baseball life—a championship team.

Vijay was already out in front of his house, waving both hands. His mitt was on his left hand, but that didn't stop Vijay. He was the king of excitement, as always.

"I can't believe it!" he said breathlessly as he plunked himself down in the seat beside Derek. "Slap me five. We're going all the way this time!"

Derek gave him five, but he wished Vijay wouldn't always make big predictions like that, at least not out loud. Derek thought it was bad luck to act like you'd already won something when you hadn't even stepped onto the field yet. In fact, neither he nor Vijay even knew who most of their teammates were!

But that was about to change. Every year at this time Derek practically held his breath as he waited to see who was on his team. But this year he was especially excited, so he could hardly blame Vijay for bursting at the seams.

In the back of the station wagon were two big duffel bags full of baseball equipment—everything the Indians would need, including balls, bats, helmets, and catcher's equipment. There were also maroon-and-gray Indians uniforms, socks, and hats in two big plastic garbage bags.

Vijay always saw the bright side of things. It was one of the main reasons Derek liked him so much.

"You boys ready to get to work?" Mr. Jeter asked them. "While it may be all fun for you, it's not all games with me and Mr. Bradway. We're going to put you through your paces. Got to be in shape if we're going to compete."

"You mean you are going to make us *exercise*?" Vijay asked. "Don't worry. We are already in shape from gym class!"

Mr. Jeter laughed. "We'll see. Coach Bradway and I were both in the army, remember? We may just put you kids through boot camp, so watch out."

They all laughed. Derek could tell that his dad was just as excited as the two boys. This was the day he would meet his first-ever team, the kids he would be responsible for all season long. It was a big job, and Derek could see that his dad, while joking around, was still taking his task very seriously.

They parked by their assigned field at Westwood Little League. The boys helped tote the equipment bags over to the home bench and lined up the bats and helmets along the fence.

"Why don't you two go toss it around for a few minutes? We're still early," said Mr. Jeter, taking out his notepad and pen. "Ah, good. Here comes Mr. Bradway."

The big Mercedes pulled up behind the Jeter station

wagon, and out scrambled Dave. Derek's mom had already dubbed the boys the Three Musketeers. Dave ran over to Derek and Vijay and got right into their game of catch.

Mr. Bradway—or "just Chase," as he instructed everyone to call him—was the Hennum family's driver, and Dave's caretaker while his parents were away on business, which was often. He got out and joined Mr. Jeter. Together they looked over their rules, schedules, and roster sheets. Practice wasn't scheduled to begin for another fifteen minutes.

Dave was as excited as everyone else. "We're riding a winner this season, guys. I can feel it."

"There is no doubt," Vijay agreed. "We are coming in first place for sure!"

"Hey, now. Let's not get overconfident," Derek warned. "We still have to play the games, remember?"

"Yeah, yeah, I know," Dave said. "But come on, Derek. Admit it. You feel it too."

It was true. Derek did have the strong feeling that they were going to be something special.

"I mean," Dave added, "it can't be for nothing that we all got on the same team again, *and* that your dad and Chase are coaching."

"It's too good to be true!" Vijay exulted.

That's just it, Derek couldn't help feeling. As psyched as he was, it did somehow feel *too* good to be true. He was only ten, but Derek already knew that life didn't usually hand out gobs of ice cream without at least a small helping of spinach on the side.

The thing that made him particularly nervous was that his dad had refused to show him the roster sheet when it had arrived in the mail the day before. "League rules," he'd said when Derek had begged to see who else was on the team. "You'll find out soon enough."

But his *dad* knew *now*, Derek thought. And that was driving him crazy.

"Hey, look. It's Harry and Josh!" Dave said, pointing. "Here they come."

"Do you think—" Vijay began hopefully. "Harry and Josh are ace players. If they are on the team, it will be fantastic!"

But they didn't stop at field number four. They waved, said "Hi," and kept on going, all the way over to field number two.

Rats, thought Derek. *That would have been so cool. . . .*

Cubby Katz jogged by and waved hello, but he wasn't on the Indians either. The speediest kid in town wound up on field number three.

"Hey! Heads up!" Dave yelled. He was in the act of throwing the ball to Derek, who had stopped paying attention in the middle of their game of catch.

Derek turned his attention back to Dave and Vijay so that he wouldn't get conked on the head. A few minutes later, when he turned to take another peek at the bench, there were a few kids gathered around his dad and Chase.

Derek recognized one of them. Jonathan Hogue was in his class at Saint Augustine's school, along with Dave and Vijay. Jonathan waved and smiled, and Derek was glad to see him. He was a nice kid, although Derek wasn't sure what kind of athlete he was. If he'd played in Little League before this, Derek had never run into him.

There were three other kids surrounding Chase, who was checking them in, then sending them over to Mr. Jeter for uniforms. "Hey!" Derek said. "If we want to get our favorite numbers, we'd better get over there!"

He sure hoped his dad had saved number 13 for him. It had been Charles Jeter's old number at college and had always been Derek's favorite for that reason.

"Did you save it for me?" he asked his dad.

"Wait your turn, Derek," Mr. Jeter said. "Go check in with Coach Bradway."

Derek was a little surprised that his dad was making him get in line like all the other kids who had just shown up. But he kind of understood. His dad liked to do things by the book, according to the rules—like not showing Derek the roster in advance.

"Hey, there's my main man!" Chase said, high-fiving Derek and checking him in. "You ready?"

"Always," Derek replied with a grin and a nod.

"Ha! That's the spirit. Okay, go get your new suit."

Derek got in line behind three other kids. He'd seen

them around in school, but he remembered only one from past seasons, a kid named Eddie Falk, who struck out a lot.

Looking around, Derek didn't see anybody from his mental wish list of teammates. One or two looked like they might be good athletes. But still Derek felt vaguely disappointed, and a little worried that the "sure thing" Vijay and Dave were imagining was starting to look a little shaky.

"There you go, Derek," said his dad, handing him uniform number 7.

"But—" Derek started.

"I know, I know," said his dad. "Thirteen is an extra large. Are you sure you still want it?"

Derek knew he was a size medium, if not small. He shook his head, disappointed again.

"Hey, number seven is Mickey Mantle's number!" Mr. Jeter pointed out. "The Mick! One of the all-time great Yankees."

That was true, Derek had to admit. There were a lot worse numbers.

"Besides, it's lucky. Lucky seven! Tell you what, Son. Whether you make your own luck, or you *need* a little luck, seven is your number." He gave Derek a smile and a wink, and Derek couldn't help smiling back as he took his uniform and hat.

"Okay, Indians!" Mr. Jeter said loudly, clapping his hands. "Let's gather round, shall we?" He introduced himself and Chase and said they were co-coaches. "Just call us both 'Coach,'" he instructed the team. "One of us will be sure to answer. Now let me have Coach Bradway read the roll call. Coach?"

"Derek Jeter?"

"Here."

"Dave Hennum?"

"Here."

"Vijay—"

"Right here!"

"Patel. . . . Jonathan Hogue. . . ."

He went on reading names. When all were accounted for, Chase said, "There are still three more names. Anybody know where Miles Kaufman is?"

Derek knew Miles. He'd been on last year's team and had improved as the season had gone on, but he was no all-star. Nice kid, though.

"Jonah Winters?"

"Here!" a kid yelled, running up to join the rest of them. He was carrying a baseball mitt like he'd never held one before.

"Gary Parnell?"

There was an audible gasp from at least three other kids besides Derek. But as for Derek himself, all he heard was the sound of a loud, terrible gong in his head. *The Gong of Doom.*

GARY PARNELL? Derek's biggest nemesis in school? The kid who beat him on nearly every test in every subject, and always, always rubbed it in? The kid who absolutely, positively hated sports, calling them a waste of a good brain and valuable time?

That Gary Parnell?

No. It couldn't be. There had to be another, some kid Derek had never met but who wasn't—

"Right here!"

That voice. It could only be . . .

"Are you Gary Parnell?" Chase asked.

"That's me. Unfortunately."

Derek turned around slowly . . . and there was his worst nightmare, being handed an Indians uniform and hat.

"Derek Jeter! As I live and breathe," said Gary. "Fancy meeting you here."

Derek stared. Gary looked as miserable as Derek felt.

"Why?" Derek whispered. "Why are you here? What are you, of all people, doing on a baseball field? I thought you hated baseball even more than you hate all other sports!"

"I do!" Gary confirmed. "I did, I do, and I always will. I'm just here to make your life intolerable."

"You're totally succeeding," Derek whispered, frowning.

"Seriously," Gary said with a sigh, "my mom is making me do it."

"Huh?"

"She's punishing me."

"For what? For getting only a ninety-nine on your last test?"

Gary smirked. "Feeble, Jeter. No. She insists I'm out of

shape and that I need to be more active. *Yecch.* All this 'active and healthy' stuff makes me want to puke." He stared at the uniform in his hands. "And they don't really expect me to dress up in *this*, do they? There is no way. Sor-ry."

This was a disaster of the highest proportions. Derek could feel the panic rising in his throat. He needed to scream—but of course that wasn't going to happen. He was just going to have to somehow overcome this . . . this catastrophe.

"Your mother is right," Derek managed to say. "You do need to get in shape. I mean, your brain might be in shape, but—"

"Yeah, yeah." Gary dismissed him. "I'll show her—and the rest of you too, while I'm at it. I'm going to use this unfortunate period of forced torture to prove once and for all that sports are a complete waste of time and belong in the dustbin of history."

Derek wanted to scream. He wanted to take an eraser and wipe this day clean so that he could start it all over and make it turn out differently.

But he couldn't do any of that. There was his dad, right over there. There was Chase. There were his friends. There were all these other kids who were going to be his teammates.

Derek knew he would have to accept this unacceptable, horrible mistake. But how in the world were he and the Indians supposed to even *contend* for a championship with *Gary Parnell* on the team?

Chapter Two
NIGHTMARE

"Okay, team, let's get going!" Mr. Jeter said, clapping his hands three times. "Don't worry about the uniforms. Just leave them here on the bench until after practice. You can save them for game action. But everyone wears a hat from here on out, practices included. We want to be able to tell the good guys from the bad guys."

He was joking, Derek knew. Some of the kids laughed a little, but most just listened. They didn't know Derek's dad the way he did. Mr. Jeter could be as funny as they come, but underneath he was always serious, and so was Derek.

That was why it made Derek furious that while his dad was addressing the team, Gary kept clowning around.

Hidden by the backs of two players who were standing

in front of him, Gary was amusing two other boys by trying—and failing—to balance the bill of his cap on his nose. The two other boys stifled their giggles so the coaches wouldn't hear, but Derek wanted to go over there and make them pay better attention.

"First things first. Coach Bradway?"

Chase stepped forward. "Okay. Everybody up on your feet. Three times around the bases, double time. Let's go, go, go!"

Vijay, Dave, Derek, and a couple of other boys led the way. Derek nearly came up on Vijay's heels by the time they reached second base, so Derek had to slow down a little. The team members settled into a moderate pace—too slow for Derek's taste, but hey, they were only getting warmed up.

He was barely winded after three times around the bases. Standing there, he could see how the rest of them were progressing. There were three or four other kids who seemed to have some speed. But there were four or five others who were distinctly as slow as molasses. And Gary, of course, was bringing up the rear, and by a wide margin. He shuffled around the bases as if he were towing a heavy load of lumber, moaning and groaning dramatically as he went.

When he finally crossed home plate for the third time, he sat down right there in the dirt. "Ow! I've got a pebble in my shoe!" he said, grimacing in terrible pain. "Can I go sit on the bench and get it out?"

Chase frowned but nodded, and Gary limped over there and sat down with a great sigh.

"You boys need to work yourselves into game shape," Mr. Jeter told them. "Ten push-ups, everybody. Drop and go!"

Derek did his push-ups, eyeing Gary's smirking face as he did so. Okay, Gary had gotten away with not doing push-ups. But how long could he keep fooling Derek's dad and Chase? Not long, Derek thought. Sooner or later they'd surely catch on to Gary's act and put a stop to it.

"Okay. I'm going to call some names out, and those I call will be in the field first. The rest will hit first, with Coach Bradway. Then we'll switch it up."

Derek's name wasn't called, although Vijay's and Dave's were. Vijay jogged out to the outfield, where he had always played in previous seasons, and Dave went to his preferred position, third base. Derek joined the other kids whose names hadn't been called as they gathered around Chase.

"I'm going to pitch to you one at a time," said Chase. "Ten swings each, and you don't have to swing at it if it's not close. It's never too soon to get a good sense of the strike zone."

There were only four batting helmets, and six kids, so Derek decided to wait and watch the others hit first. Glancing to his left, he saw that Gary Parnell was still sitting on the bench. His left shoe was off, and he seemed to be examining the bottom of his sock with great interest.

"Didn't my dad call your name?" Derek asked him.

"I don't know," Gary said. "I wasn't listening."

"What is that, a boulder you've got in there?" Derek asked, sitting down next to him.

Gary laughed. "I didn't have a rock in my shoe, you dummy. I just needed a break."

"A break?" Derek repeated. "Are you kidding? We've barely gotten started!"

"Yeah, well, *I'm done*. These stupid shoes are killing me. What are these ridiculous things on the bottoms, anyway?"

"Those are cleats," Derek explained. "But don't play dumb with me. You know that already."

"Who, me?" Gary said, grinning.

"Listen, even if you don't care, you should have some respect for the rest of us who do."

Gary snorted. "Why? Just because you're all crazy doesn't mean I have to feed your delusions."

Derek couldn't think of a comeback for that one, but he decided it wasn't worth wasting any more time on Gary. Anyway, it was Derek's turn to hit.

The kid ahead of him had hit some nice line drives, Derek noted. A big, strong kid who looked in decent shape. "Nice hitting," Derek told him as he took the kid's place at the plate. "I'm Derek."

"Paul Edwards," the boy replied, shaking hands. "You're Coach's son?"

"Yup. That's my dad out there with the fielders."

"Nice. Seems like a cool couple of coaches. Too bad about that jerk on the bench." He nodded toward Gary.

"Oh him," Derek said, managing a smile. "Well, what are you gonna do?"

He stepped up to the plate and proceeded to mash a succession of pitches to every area of the field.

When he was done, he heard applause from the bench. "Very good!" Gary said. "You've succeeded in life. That and a dollar will get you bus fare. Congratulations."

Derek bit down hard on his lip and on his impulse to make Gary cut it out once and for all.

Instead Derek tried to concentrate on silver linings. For the rest of the practice, as he went full tilt the way he always did, he looked around at the rest of the Indians, searching for signs of hope and promise.

He found a few, although over all, the team looked like it needed a lot of work—the kind of work his dad and Chase would be good at making them do, luckily.

On the plus side there was Paul Edwards's hitting, Jonathan Hogue's arm, Mason Adams's and Dean O'Leary's speed, Tito Ortega's power potential. And of course there were Dave and Vijay, who had already been to the batting cages with Derek and his dad more than once, and whose hitting showed the benefits.

All in all, not the worst team Derek had ever been on, at least in terms of potential. But the Indians certainly had a long, long way to go.

Worst of all, they had an instant and huge attitude problem with Gary. As practice went on, Gary continued to loaf, goof off, and make cracks, which two other players, Eddie and Jonah, seemed to find endlessly funny. Chase and Mr. Jeter were continually having to call the team to attention.

Now Gary was getting laughs by trying—and failing repeatedly—to tie the extra long laces on his cleats, which were brand-new and had obviously never been worn before today. Eddie and Jonah seemed to find all this hilarious, to the point of imitating Gary's antics themselves.

Finally Derek lost it and whispered for them to cut it out.

"Derek!" his dad called out sternly. "I don't need you competing with me for everyone's attention. Snap to it and pay attention. This is important."

Derek could feel his face turn red as Gary softly sniggered and a few other team members giggled at Derek's discomfort.

Derek sat there, steaming. It was *Gary's* fault that Derek had gotten distracted! Why couldn't his dad see that? Why was he blaming Derek and not Gary?

It was all so unfair!

On the other side Paul, Miles, Tito, and a few others, sharing Derek's frustration, were busy cracking jokes and making negative comments about Gary.

The net result was that there was a lot of talking and

fooling around while the coaches were trying to run practice. Chase and Mr. Jeter were constantly having to command the boys' attention—repeating themselves and wasting valuable time that could have been spent improving the team's baseball skills.

As Derek watched the Indians' precious practice time tick away, his frustration mounted to an almost unbearable level. He began to fantasize ways his dad could get Gary off the team, but those fantasies only served to take his own attention away from baseball!

Derek desperately wanted to talk to his dad, to tell him about Gary and make his dad crack down before Gary wrecked everything. But there was no opportunity. Mr. Jeter was totally busy the whole time, working with each and every kid on the team—including Gary—trying to correct this or that aspect of their game.

In the car on the way home, Vijay, enthusiastic as usual, did a lot of talking about how they were going to win this year. "Paul is going to hit a hundred home runs! He's so big and strong! And Tito, too! We're going to score so many runs!"

Never mind that Tito swung with his eyes closed, or that Paul's swing was wild and all arms. But that was okay. His dad could fix those kinds of things over time.

It was the *other* stuff that really bothered Derek, but this was obviously not the time to mention it. He would have to wait until later—maybe at dinner, after he and his dad had both had a chance to reflect on the day and the team's first practice.

"My team is going to win the championship!" Derek's little sister, Sharlee, was practically bouncing up and down in her chair, she was so excited. "Me and Ciara are the best players in the whole league!"

"Ciara and *I*," Mrs. Jeter corrected her.

"Whatever."

"No, not 'whatever,' Sharlee," said Mr. Jeter. "It's important to use good grammar."

"What's grammar?" Sharlee asked.

She was only in first grade, so her confusion was understandable, thought Derek. Anyway, she was so sweet and cute that he couldn't help smiling at her antics. Sharlee was a good athlete, too—exceptional for her age—and so was her new best friend at school, Ciara.

"Ciara says I'm as good a hitter as Babe Ruth!" Sharlee said, in a way that showed she believed it.

"Well, you may have one or two things to learn yet," Mrs. Jeter said, giving Derek a secret wink.

"Daddy," Sharlee said, "how come you're coaching Derek and not me?"

"Now, Sharlee, we talked about this, remember?" Mr. Jeter said. "You'll get your turn. I promised I would coach you sometime, and I will. You'll just have to be patient. I am not able to coach both teams at once."

"Why not?"

"That's enough now, honey," Mrs. Jeter said. "We've already talked about this a number of times."

They had too. All year both Derek and Sharlee had been begging their dad to coach them. But Mr. Jeter had a new job now, and it took up a lot of his time and energy. Their mom worked full-time too. Otherwise she could have coached Sharlee's team.

"Mom, can I stay overnight at Ciara's?" Sharlee asked, suddenly changing the subject.

"Jeter?" Mrs. Jeter asked her husband.

"I don't know," he said, cocking his head to one side. "You're a little young for overnights, Sharlee."

"I'm not young! I'm seven—well, almost."

Derek had to stop himself from laughing, especially with a mouthful of mac and cheese. Sharlee said the darnedest things sometimes.

"I think it would be all right," Mrs. Jeter assured her husband. "Ciara's a terrific kid. And weren't her parents such nice, friendly folks?"

"Yes, they were," Mr. Jeter agreed. "Well, if you think so—"

"Yay!" Sharlee said, clapping. "Happyhappyhappy!"

They all laughed, but it got Derek thinking. He and Dave had been talking about an overnight themselves, and for quite a while. But since Dave's parents were always traveling, Mr. and Mrs. Jeter hadn't met them yet. And as much as the Jeters liked Chase, he was only Dave's caretaker and driver, not a parent—and that meant no overnights, at least until Dave's parents met Derek's, and met with the Jeters' approval.

Derek thought again about today's practice, and how upset he still felt that Gary was on his team. He couldn't picture an entire season of Gary tormenting him with his snide, negative comments and stupid attempts at humor.

"Derek?" his mom asked. "Everything okay? You're so quiet all of a sudden."

"I'm fine," he said, not wanting to spoil everybody's good mood.

"You sure?" she asked.

"Uh-huh," he grunted, digging into another mouthful of mac and cheese.

"All right, then," she said.

"Can we call Ciara's mom now and tell her I'm sleeping over?" Sharlee asked eagerly.

Mrs. Jeter laughed. "You're not sleeping over tonight, honey. But I'll tell you what. If you help me with the dishes, I'll call her when we're done."

"Why doesn't Derek have to help?"

"He's going to, when he's done eating," their mom answered. "Right, Derek? You do the drying?"

"Mmph," Derek mumbled, nodding, his mouth still full.

"There. See?" Mrs. Jeter said. "Around this house everybody pitches in. Come on, big girl. You can tell me all about your home runs."

They went into the kitchen, leaving Derek and his dad alone at the table. After a moment Mr. Jeter said, "All right. What's going on in that mind of yours, Derek? I can smell the wood burning."

Derek swallowed his food, sighed, and said, "Dad, why does Gary have to be on our team?"

Mr. Jeter opened his eyes wide. "Did I just hear you right? Are you asking me to kick somebody off the team?"

Derek sighed again. "Dad, he—"

"Derek, it's no crime to be weak at sports. You know very well that rosters are drawn up by the league. I couldn't change that even if I wanted to, and I *don't* want to."

"It's not that he stinks at baseball," Derek said. "It's—"

"Yes? Come on, let's hear it."

"He's . . . he's always annoying people!"

"Annoying *you*, you mean."

"And a lot of other kids! Didn't you see how he—"

"I'm going to stop you right there, old man," said Mr. Jeter. "You asked me to coach your team, and that's what I'm going to do. Every kid on my team is just as import-ant and valuable to me as any other, and that includes you. If there's a problem on the team, you just let Chase and me handle it. Derek, you need to focus on what you can control, instead of worrying about things you can't. If you don't like the situation, figure out what *you* can do to improve it."

"But, Dad—"

"No buts. You just work hard at your own game and be the best teammate you can be. Chase and I will take care of the rest. Now go help your mom and Sharlee with the dishes." So saying, Mr. Jeter got up from the table and left the room.

Derek stifled the urge to complain some more—it was no use anyway, he knew—and got up from the table. As he did, his dad poked his head back into the room.

"By the way, Derek, have you read through your contract lately?"

"I guess it's been a while. . . . Why?"

"Because it says in there, as I recall, that you promise to be a good teammate and show respect for your coaches. Check it out—and think about it."

Derek helped with the dishes, only half-listening as his mom and sister happily chatted about T-ball and overnights, first grade and kiddie birthday parties. But inside he was feeling deeply troubled. His dad had just given him a first-class talking-to, and Derek still felt stung.

His mom noticed, he could tell. But she was sensitive enough not to bring it up with him while Sharlee was there.

Later that evening, though, when he was in bed with the lights out, his mom knocked on his bedroom door. "Come in," he said.

She sat down on the edge of his bed and said, "Come on,

old man. Let's have it. What's getting you down? I haven't seen you this upset in a long time."

Derek sat up and said, "Mom, Dad won't listen! Our team is going to stink this year, and Dad won't even try to fix it. Everything is ruined!"

She leaned forward and hugged him. "Oh, now, Derek, you don't mean that. How can you be so sure, anyway? Today was only the first practice. You've got the whole season ahead of you."

"I know!" he said. "That's what's so terrible. I had all these dreams of a perfect season with Dad as my coach, and now he won't even listen to me. He says I should just look to my own game and let him take care of the team."

"And he's right," Mrs. Jeter said. "That's his job."

"But he doesn't realize! And by the time he does, it'll be too late."

"Hey, don't bury the team before you've even played one game," she told him.

"You don't understand, Mom. There's this kid on the team—"

"Derek, it's a *team* sport. One member can't sink the whole season all by himself."

"You don't know Gary," he said miserably.

"Gary? Isn't he your friend from school?"

"Friend? More like worst enemy."

"Derek, stop it now. You're too young to have enemies. And that's no way to look at things." She paused for a moment, thinking. "Ah, I remember now. He's the boy who's always getting the best grades in class, right?"

"Uh-huh. And he's always shoving it in my face too."

"Well, nobody's perfect. But if you're going to be on the same team—"

"You don't understand, Mom," Derek insisted. "Gary's going to wreck everything. He hates sports, and he hates me!"

"I'm sure you're exaggerating, Derek."

"I'm not. He spent the entire practice fooling around and being annoying—and Dad didn't do anything about it."

His mom took him by the shoulders and looked him right in the eye. "Derek," she said. "I appreciate you sharing your feelings with me. But you've got to give your dad some time, *and* some slack. Remember, he's your dad, not everyone else's. He can't just deal with them as if they were you."

"But—"

"Coaches have a lot to do, old man, and you've got to trust Dad and Chase to get it done."

"But if he doesn't get Gary off the team soon, we're going to lose!"

"Derek, you know your father couldn't do that, not even if he wanted to. And he wouldn't anyway. You've got to remember, Little League is for everyone who wants to play, not just for the good athletes."

"It's not just that he stinks at baseball. It's that he hates sports!"

"Derek, I can understand how you feel," Mrs. Jeter said gently. "But I have to say, I think Dad was right when he said to just take care of your own game. He's pretty good at problem solving, but he's got to concentrate on the whole team, and he needs to be able to count on you giving it your best."

"But, Mom—"

"What did I just say?" She stopped him. "Trust your dad, and trust Chase. And remember, Rome wasn't built in a day."

After giving him a kiss on the forehead, she got up and went to the door. "Try to get some sleep, all right, old man? And trust your father."

"Thanks, Mom," Derek said. "I'll think about it."

"G'night," she said, blowing him a kiss and closing the door.

Derek lay there in the dark, thinking over what she'd said. He felt somewhat better. His mom was right, of course—as usual. It was ridiculous for him to doubt his dad. There was no better coach in the world. If Derek's dad couldn't make things better, nobody could.

Still, Gary's attitude was one thing even his dad might not be able to fix.

Derek lay there in the dark, unable to sleep, and still feeling troubled, in spite of his mom's soothing words. This was supposed to be the greatest day of his life. Why did Gary, of all people in the world, have to end up on Derek's team?

Chapter Three
PRANKS AND PUZZLES

"Okay, get two! Two!"

Mr. Jeter hit the ball on the ground to Derek at shortstop. Derek scooped it up, wheeled, and fired to Mason, who stepped on second and whipped it to Tito at first. It would have been a great double play *if* they'd been playing a real game.

But this was only practice, of course—the team's second in three days, and only two days before their first game of the season. Chase and Mr. Jeter had started the day with fielding drills, and Derek was right where he felt most comfortable, at short.

Tito threw the ball in to Chase, who stood near the plate with his mitt on, and Chase handed it back to Mr. Jeter so that he could hit another.

This was better than their first practice. *Much better,* Derek thought. Since his conversation with his mom the other night, he'd made up his mind to concentrate only on positive thoughts and banish any negative ones from his mind. To be fair, it was easier today because, as of yet, Gary hadn't shown up for practice.

Maybe he's convinced his mom to let him quit the team! Derek stopped himself from fantasizing about it. It would have been too good to be true if Gary weren't on the team anymore. But that, he knew, was a negative thought.

Be a good teammate, he reminded himself, reciting the clause in the contract he'd signed with his parents.

His contract was incredibly important to Derek. His whole life's dream—to play shortstop for the New York Yankees someday—depended on his fulfilling his contract. His parents had agreed to back him fully and completely, but only if Derek kept his part of the bargain.

The contract, which they'd agreed to after much hard bargaining, had some hard-to-keep items on it, and this was proving to be one of them.

"Okay, heads up in the outfield. Cutoff men, get ready!" Mr. Jeter hit one high and far. Vijay backed up on it, but Dean called for it, and Vijay backed off, even though the ball was closer to him and should have been his.

Dean fired it back in to Derek, who had jogged out into short left field to take the throw. After grabbing it, he quickly pivoted and threw a strike in to Chase.

"Attaway!" Chase shouted, pointing his mitt at Derek to indicate what a good job he'd done. Then Chase flipped the ball back to Mr. Jeter.

"Men on first and second, nobody out. Get ready for the bunt!" Mr. Jeter yelled.

Derek knew his job was to cover third base if the bunt went that way, second base if the ball went toward first. He bounced up and down on the balls of his feet, ready for either option.

Just as Mr. Jeter was about to throw the ball into the air, a car pulled up to the curb and Gary got out.

Rats! thought Derek. He'd shown up after all. Then Derek stopped himself again, realizing he was being negative. But it was *so hard* not to be when Gary was around!

"You're late," Chase told Gary.

"Sorry," Gary said. "I had to go to the doctor. For my asthma."

"You have asthma?" Mr. Jeter asked. "It wasn't on your application form."

"Um . . . oh, yeah. I forgot to add it in. . . ."

"Are you okay to practice, son?"

"I guess," Gary said, sounding unsure.

"Well, go ahead out to left." Mr. Jeter signaled to Vijay. "Come on in, Vij!"

Vijay ran in, while Gary walked out to the outfield, taking his sweet time. Clearly, thought Derek, Gary had no intention of breaking a sweat today, or any other day, for that matter.

As Gary passed him at short, Derek said, "Since when do you have asthma?"

Gary looked at Derek as if he were stupid, and let out a snort. "Get real," he said, and kept walking.

Derek shook his head. Obviously Gary would say or do *anything* to avoid playing baseball. Derek wondered what his dad would do if he realized Gary had just lied to his face.

When Mr. Jeter hit Gary a fly ball, Gary barely moved, and Dean had to race over to make the grab. "Good hustle!" Chase shouted. Dean waved back—and so did Gary! As if he'd even moved a muscle to try to catch the ball.

"Good hustle!" Dean repeated mockingly to Gary. "Next time maybe stick your glove out at least."

Gary gave him a smarmy smile, but he clearly had no intention of doing any such thing.

When drills were finished, the coaches divided the teams into two groups for a short scrimmage.

Sitting on the bench with Gary and three others, waiting for their chance to hit, Derek heard the sound of giggles coming from the other kids seated nearby. Looking up, he saw that they were all looking at *him*.

"What?" he asked.

Eddie dissolved into giggles, and so did Jonah. That made Derek mad.

"What? What are you laughing at?"

Laughing so hard that tears were coming out of his eyes,

Jonah pointed to Derek's baseball cap. Derek reached up and took it off. There, on the top of it where the button sat, someone had stuck a large wad of bubble gum!

"Eeeuw!" Derek said, grimacing as he tried to remove it without his fingers getting stuck to the gooey mess. Strings of gum stayed stuck to his cap, even after he'd gotten the big mass off. Everyone was laughing now—including Dean, who just a little while ago had seemed as angry at Gary as Derek was.

Derek glared at Gary, who returned his stare with an innocent *Who, me?* look.

"Derek!" his dad called. "Wake up over there!"

"Huh?" Derek turned around to see his dad holding up a bat.

"You're up. Let's go! We don't have all day to waste here."

"Dad, Gary was—"

"Let's go, let's go!" his dad said.

"But—"

"Not now, Derek. Come on. Quit wasting everyone's time."

Derek sighed, seeing it was no use. Glancing over to the bench, he saw Gary, thumbs in his ears, wiggling his fingers and sticking his tongue out at him.

Derek grabbed his bat, marched to the plate, and turned to face Chase, who was pitching for both sides. The ball came in, and Derek swung right out of his shoes, trying to send the ball all the way to Mars.

Of course he missed completely, and from there his frustration only grew.

Worse was that right after he'd struck out on three pathetic overswings, Gary stepped up to the plate and hit a pop-up that fell in behind third base for a hit!

"Attaway!" Mr. Jeter called out, applauding. "Nice going, Gary."

On the next hit Gary was thrown out at second because he practically walked over there instead of hustling. But the coaches didn't give him a hard time about it. *Of course not,* thought Derek. Because the poor kid had *asthma* and had just come from the doctor—*supposedly.*

But Derek had been in class with Gary for three years now. If he had asthma, he'd been hiding it awfully well. And Derek doubted that Gary's lateness had been on account of his going to the doctor. He'd probably tried to argue his way out of coming, hoping that by the time his mom forced him to go, practice would already be over.

Out in the field Derek kept hearing Gary's snide, stupid comments coming from behind him in left. Gary was smart enough to make his voice loud enough for Derek to hear but not so loud that the coaches would hear, since they were farther away.

Derek glanced over at Dave, who was manning third. Dave scowled and shook his head. Derek was glad that at least one other person shared his frustration.

As Vijay stood at the plate, about to swing at one of Chase's pitches, Gary called, "Heads up!"

Derek turned his head, just as Vijay made contact. The ball came straight for Derek, and he muffed what should have been an easy catch.

"Grrrr!" he growled behind clenched teeth.

"Come on. Wake up out there at short!" his dad called from behind home plate.

Derek steamed, and got back into "ready position." Couldn't his dad see what Gary was doing? Couldn't Chase see it? They sure seemed not to. Instead both were totally focused on improving the team's skills, and were completely oblivious to the real problem, namely *Gary Parnell*!

Derek made two more errors in the space of ten minutes, both caused by Gary's distracting him.

"Derek!" His dad walked out toward short. "Come here."

Uh-oh.

"What's going on with you, Derek? Are you here or somewhere else?"

"Dad, Gary's—"

"Stop it right there," Mr. Jeter told him. "Don't give me excuses. Who's responsible for you?"

"But—"

"Who?"

Derek sighed. "I am."

"That's right. Now go out and play center field for a while." He whistled for Dean to come in and play shortstop.

Derek couldn't believe it. His own dad, making him play the outfield!

Even though he knew every position was important, being put in the outfield felt like banishment to Derek, who had almost always played shortstop—or at least in the infield, where there was always lots of action.

Why was his dad punishing him, *and in front of everyone on the team*?

Derek knew his dad would never do anything to hurt him, but he also knew that his dad didn't ever put up with bad behavior. Mr. Jeter must have thought it was Derek who was distracting the team members—but it *wasn't*! How could his dad be so taken in by Gary's shenanigans?

With Gary right next to him in left field, the stupid comments kept coming, and Derek couldn't wait for practice to be over. In all his life he had never thought there would come a moment when he didn't want to be playing baseball. This should have been his moment in the sun, but Gary was totally ruining it for him!

"What happened out there today, Derek?" his dad wanted to know. They'd just dropped Vijay off and were parking the car in front of the family's townhouse. "You didn't seem like yourself."

"It wasn't my fault," Derek replied. "Didn't you see what Gary—"

"I see everything I need to see," said Mr. Jeter. "I see

that it's easy to distract you from your purpose. That's not good. I'm trying to teach you to be focused, to the point where nobody and nothing can distract you. That's why I put you in the outfield. To make you realize how important focus is. And to make everyone else on the team understand that Chase and I won't put up with goofing around from anyone, not even my own son."

Derek was silent for a long moment. He wanted to tell his dad everything Gary had done to wreck things. He wanted to ask why his dad and Chase hadn't stopped all the fooling around.

But he couldn't say a word. Not without breaking his contract. He knew how his dad would see that sort of whining. He'd see it as not being a good teammate or respecting your coaches.

Derek could see how that was true. Good teammates didn't complain about one another. And like his dad had said, if Derek couldn't keep his attention where it belonged, that was up to *him* to fix, not his dad or anyone else. Still, the whole situation didn't seem fair somehow. . . .

"You know," Mr. Jeter said, turning off the engine and removing the keys, "sometimes things don't go the way we expect them to, and we have to make adjustments. I want you to know I have confidence in you. You can be the heart and soul of this team, if you manage to get yourself back on track. It's up to you."

"Okay, Dad," Derek said, nodding. "I've got it. I will."

"Good man. Now let's go wash up for supper."

The next day at school Derek found he was once again having trouble concentrating, which was a big problem, since Ms. Fein started their day by handing out a surprise test in social studies.

Derek looked over at Gary, who was busy scribbling away, writing his answers down. He seemed to be having no problem with the subject matter.

Derek, on the other hand, was so upset about Gary and the way he'd set out to ruin Derek's entire baseball season, that he could barely concentrate.

He forced himself to pay attention to the questions, but when he finally handed the test in, just before time was up, he was afraid he'd messed up badly. That, too, was a no-no in his contract, which clearly stated that he had to get good grades if he wanted to play sports.

As the students were all shuffling out of the classroom on their way to lunch, Gary moved close to Derek and muttered, "Hey there, Jeter."

"What do you want?" Derek could barely contain his anger.

"I just wanted to say, I was wrong about baseball."

"Huh?" Derek was taken aback. Was Gary actually admitting he'd been wrong all this time?

"Yeah," Gary said with a sigh. "It's even worse than I

thought. Way, way worse. In fact, it's the dumbest activity on the planet."

Far from admitting he was wrong, Gary was taking his annoyingness to a new, higher level!

"Very funny. Oh, and by the way, if you have asthma, where's your inhaler?"

Gary made a face, as if Derek had just said something immensely stupid. "Are you kidding? I'd say anything—*anything*—if it meant I didn't have to play your stupid sport."

"You lied to my dad—right to his face!"

"Yeah? And what are you going to do about it? Go ahead, get yourself suspended, smart guy." He spread his arms out wide, daring Derek to shove him, or worse.

Derek resisted the temptation. "Okay, okay," he said. "You win. Have it your way. I hope it makes you happy to make everyone else on the team miserable."

"Not everyone. Just you," Gary replied with a smirk. "In fact, I've noticed that more than a few of the kids seem to find my humor enjoyable."

There was no sense talking with Gary, Derek realized. So he just turned away and headed for the cafeteria, where he plunked himself down at the table that Dave and Vijay were already sitting at, digging into their pizza.

"What's up?" Dave asked. "You look kind of bummed out."

"I am," Derek admitted. "How would you feel if you

were me and your dad made you move to the outfield?"

"Yes. Why ever did he do that?" Vijay asked. "It was very strange to see."

"It was Gary's fault," Derek explained. "I got distracted, but my dad didn't see what happened, so he thought it was me goofing around."

"Well, don't worry," Vijay said. "I am sure you will play shortstop in the real games. Your dad is the best coach in the whole wide world, and so is Chase. They will always make the right decisions for the team."

"He's right," Dave said. "Didn't you see how they were working with all those kids? And a lot of them need it. You can't really blame your dad and Chase if they don't see what Gary's up to. I mean, they're pretty busy, and he's pretty good at hiding it from them."

Then Derek told them what Gary had just said about his supposed asthma, and as Derek had expected, both of them were as outraged as he was.

"Did you tell your dad?" Vijay asked. "I bet if you do, he kicks Gary right off the team!"

"I don't know," Derek said, shaking his head. "I have a feeling he wouldn't."

"You should tell him anyway," Dave said.

"I tried. He didn't want to hear any complaining."

"I'm going to tell Chase," Dave said. "Somebody's got to do *something* about that kid, before he starts costing us wins on the field."

"Yes indeed!" Vijay agreed. "The first game is tomorrow. If we don't get him off the team before that, he will destroy our chance to be champions!"

Exactly, thought Derek, though he didn't say so out loud. Well, maybe telling Chase would work, but Derek had a feeling Dave would get the same response: "Stop complaining, take care of your own business, and leave the coaching to the coaches."

Chapter Four

MORE SURPRISES

"Ciara, tell my daddy what we both did today!"

Sharlee sat at the Jeters' dinner table, practically bouncing up and down in her chair. Her new best friend and current T-ball teammate, Ciara, a cute red-haired girl who was always giggling, sat next to her.

"We both hit home runs!" Ciara chirped, and the two girls high-fived.

"Yessss!" Sharlee cried. "We already won our first two games, and we're never gonna lose, ever!"

Derek sat across from them, trying to eat his spaghetti despite his sudden loss of appetite. He was happy for Sharlee—really, he was—but he would have been a lot happier if things had been going better in his own baseball life.

"Mommy saw the whole game!" Sharlee went on. "Right, Mom?"

"Uh-huh, yes I did," said Mrs. Jeter. "It was super. You guys both rocked. But if you don't eat your supper, you won't be strong enough to hit any more homers. Right, old man?" She turned and gave Derek a wink.

He smiled as best he could and said, "That's right, Sharlee." Normally his words would have had a lot more enthusiasm behind them, but Derek just couldn't work it up. Not tonight.

Inside he was churning with anxiety about the team's first game tomorrow.

"Are you okay, old man?" his mom asked.

Derek looked down at his plate. Nothing ever got by her. "I'm fine," he insisted. "Fine."

"Hmmm," Mrs. Jeter replied. Derek looked up in time to see her exchange a meaningful glance with his dad. "Not hungry tonight, slugger?" she asked.

"I guess not," he said. "I'm kind of tired. Big day tomorrow. . . . I think I'll go up to my room."

Mrs. Jeter glanced at the two little girls, who were having a grand old time making each other giggle. "Derek, if you're done eating, why don't you come help me do the dishes?"

He knew what that meant. She wanted to talk to him. *Alone.*

He followed her into the kitchen and got a towel so he could start drying the dishes as she finished washing them. "So," she began almost right away, "you want to tell me what's on your mind? Or are you going to make me guess?"

Derek sighed. It was like both his parents had eyes in the backs of their heads. They knew everything that was going on with him, almost as soon as he did.

"It's Dad," he said. "I thought he was going to be the coach I always dreamed of. But so far it's not turning out that way."

"Mm-hmm," she said. "Like, for instance?"

"For instance, he thought I was clowning around—and it wasn't even me; it was Gary—so he made me play the outfield the whole rest of practice! I hardly got one ball hit to me the whole time, and Dad *knows* I'm a *shortstop*! How does he expect me to get better at it if I'm stuck in the outfield, not getting any action at all?"

"Hey, was Willie Mays 'stuck' out there? Or Mickey Mantle? Or Babe Ruth?"

"That's not the point, Mom! Dad knows I want to play short! He's just trying to punish me."

Mrs. Jeter handed him another dish to dry. "Maybe he's thinking it makes you a better player to get experience at every position. Maybe he was trying to remind you what a privilege it is to play shortstop, captain of the whole infield. Captains have to set a good example."

Funny, Derek thought. His dad had said almost the same thing. "But the whole reason it happened is because of Gary!" Derek said. "And neither Dad nor Chase did any-thing to him!"

"They didn't put him in the outfield?"

"He already plays there."

"Or bench him?"

"That would have just been doing Gary a favor," Derek said glumly. "He hates sports, remember?"

"Oh, right. You did mention that."

"He even lied about having asthma, to explain why he couldn't run drills like the rest of us!"

Mrs. Jeter opened her eyes wide. "*Really?* Are you *sure*? Maybe you just didn't know he had it."

"I've been in class with him three straight years," Derek said. "He's never even used an inhaler. And besides, when I called him on it, he pretty much admitted it right to my face!"

"I see. *Hmmm.* . . ."

"So he sits there on the bench and makes farting noises, and puts bubble gum on my hat and ruins it, and makes jokes about how stupid all the kids look in their uniforms, and stuff like that. And half the kids laugh at him!"

"*At* him, or *with* him?" Mrs. Jeter asked.

"Who knows, who cares? They're not paying attention to baseball! And Dad and Chase don't even notice! All Dad does is punish me instead!" Derek threw the dish towel onto the floor angrily and folded his arms across his chest.

His mom shut the water off and gave him a stern look.

"Sorry," he said, and bent down to pick up the towel. He handed it to her so she could dry her hands.

"You know, Derek, your dad's a pretty wise person. Maybe he trusts you boys to figure out a solution for yourselves."

"Huh? How can we do that?"

"Well, old man, let's see. . . . How can you yourself make sure your team plays up to its potential?" Patting his shoulder, she said, "I've got to go make sure those girls don't laugh themselves silly."

Smiling, she left him there to think about what she'd said.

It was a lot to digest. And right now, with their big first game looming, Derek felt overwhelmed with it all. After all, he was only eleven—well, in a month and a half, anyway. How was he supposed to be able to come up with all the answers for himself?

Derek's dad had called for the team to arrive at the field an hour early so that he and Chase could give them some extra attention. Chase was doing fielding drills with most of the kids, while Mr. Jeter helped Gary, Eddie, Jonah, and a couple of others with their swings.

From the start of the first practice, the two coaches had approached their team as teachers. There had been no talk of winning games or getting pumped up for the competition the season would soon bring.

But to Derek, baseball skills were only one part of a winning team. Another part, and just as important, was team spirit. And so far the Indians' spirit was all messed up. Half the kids were sore at Gary and his high jinks, while the other half enjoyed them. It might not have mattered in practice, but what about in games?

"Okay, Indians. Gather round," said Mr. Jeter, calling everybody over to the bench. The Cubs had arrived, and it was their turn to warm up on the field.

"Coach Bradway is going to read off the starting lineup for today," Mr. Jeter continued when everyone was paying attention. Even Gary seemed interested at the moment— probably to make sure he didn't have to play right away, thought Derek.

"Just because you aren't starting doesn't mean you won't get in the game," Mr. Jeter went on. "And it doesn't mean you won't start next time. If you're at a different position than you expect, it doesn't mean that won't change next game, or the game after."

He didn't look at Derek as he said it, but Derek was afraid those words applied to him. Was his dad really going to stick him in the outfield? *For real?*

"Coach Bradway and I want you boys to experience as many aspects of the game as possible. That'll make you better ballplayers down the road. So no matter where you are in the batting order, or in the field, or on the bench, remember, you're there for a reason, and you're there to give it your best. All right. That's my two cents. Coach Bradway?"

Chase stepped up and began. "Batting first, and playing second base, Mason. Batting second, playing center field, Dean. Batting third, and catching, Derek."

"What?" Derek was so shocked that he shouted it out loud. Immediately he wished he hadn't. He could feel his dad's stern look, even though he didn't return it.

Catcher? Catcher, of all positions?

It immediately occurred to Derek that his mom must have mentioned to his dad what he'd said about the outfield not getting enough action. His dad had obviously responded by putting him at a position where you were in the middle of things on every single pitch!

It wasn't shortstop, but it was better, at least, than being stuck in the outfield and waiting pitch after pitch for a ball to be hit your way.

On the other hand he'd never caught a game before. That made him think of what his mom had said last night, and what his dad had just repeated, about learning all aspects of the game. It made sense to Derek—sort of—but it didn't make him happy, that was for sure. He wanted to be a shortstop, and nothing but a shortstop!

Chapter Five

PLAY BALL!

So his dad had put him behind the plate. Well, Derek would show him that he could play catcher, and play it well. He'd done it before in practice and on Jeter's Hill, in pickup games with his buddies. And his dad had shown him a few basics, but Derek never thought he was going to have to apply them to a real game setting.

As he squatted down and started warming up Dave, who was today's starting pitcher, Derek realized that his dad had switched around a lot of kids, not just him.

Derek knew his dad was serious about the team members learning all the various aspects of the game. But Derek also guessed that his dad hadn't really decided who on the team belonged where. Some coaches would have just put their kids at certain positions and left them there for the whole season. Not Charles Jeter.

Dave really had some zip on his pitches today, Derek noted. As padded as the catcher's mitt was, it still hurt his palm every time a fastball whacked in there. *Got to learn to catch it in the webbing,* Derek told himself, adjusting the unfamiliar glove.

Things started off well, as Dave made the first Cubs batter strike out swinging. In the process, though, the hitter fouled two pitches off Derek—one off his mask and one off his chest pad.

Ouch! Derek hadn't realized that the padding and a mask didn't make him bulletproof. *It's tough being a catcher,* he said to himself. On the one hand you were in on every pitch. On the other hand you were going to get more than your share of bumps and bruises—and squatting down was already starting to feel uncomfortable.

Then, for some reason, Dave seemed to lose sight of the strike zone. He walked the next two Cubs hitters, on four pitches each. Derek kept trying to show him the open catcher's mitt as a target, but it didn't seem to matter.

Now the cleanup man came up. Dave, trying at all costs to get it over the plate, threw a fat pitch, not too fast and right down the middle—and the kid creamed it, way over Gary's head! Gary jogged after it, in no particular hurry, but it wouldn't have mattered anyway.

Derek stood, removed his mask, and watched three

runners score on the easy home run. The game was still in the top of the first, and the Indians were already down 3–0!

Derek walked slowly out to the mound, and saw that his dad was on his way there too. Meanwhile, Chase clapped and shouted encouragement to the rest of the team, who looked as if they needed it badly.

"Okay, let's not get all bent out of shape here," Mr. Jeter told Dave. "He just got lucky there. You've got good zip on your fastball. Just keep throwing it, and get it over. Don't worry if they make contact. You've got some fielders out there."

Except I'm *not out there!* Derek thought. Jonathan was at short, and Derek only hoped he would catch any hard shot that came to him.

Dave did what Mr. Jeter had told him to. He got a quick out on a line drive to center, where Dean hauled it in. Then Dave struck out the next batter for the final out of the inning.

"Yesss!" Derek cried as he got to his feet. "That-a-way!" he told his friend, slapping him on the back with his catcher's mitt.

"I stink," Dave said dejectedly as he took a seat on the bench.

"You do not!" Derek said. "Like my dad said, that guy got lucky."

"And I walked the two guys ahead of him."

"Never mind. We're going to get those runs back for you, starting right now," Derek promised.

The Indians came to bat ready to swing. Mason lined out, but Dean doubled down the third-base line. That brought Derek to the plate. He'd been watching the Cubs' pitcher, noticing that he threw really hard but that every pitch was in the same place—high and over the plate.

Derek decided that if the first pitch was there, he would put his best swing on it. And he did. The ball sailed over the center fielder's head and kept on going! Derek sped around the bases, and didn't stop until he slid into home, one step ahead of the relay throw!

That made it 3–2, Cubs, and the Indians whooped it up as Derek returned to the bench. Glancing over at his dad, he saw that Mr. Jeter, too, was jumping up and down, as excited as any of the kids.

Derek grinned. It was hard to remember sometimes, when his dad was being tough on him, that deep down Mr. Jeter cared about Derek as a dad does, not just as a coach.

Dave stepped up to the plate, ready to swing for the fences. He nearly came out of his shoes swinging at the first pitch—with his eyes closed, no less. And to Derek's shock, he actually hit it right on the nose. Dave scooted all the way around the bases with a long homer to tie the game!

"Woo-hoo!" Everyone joined in the shouting—except Gary, who was too busy yawning.

Derek clapped Dave on the shoulder and said, "Way to get those runs back!"

The Cubs' pitcher was rattled now, and he walked the next two Indians before Jonathan grounded out. Vijay then walked to load the bases with two down. And up to the plate, in a huge situation, came Gary.

"Strike one!" yelled the umpire as Gary let a fat pitch go right by him.

"Swing at it!" called a few of the Indians.

"Boys . . . ," Chase said sternly, and they sat back down.

Gary swung at the next pitch, which was way over his head. Of course he missed, and some of the team members groaned. "You said to swing," Gary said with a shrug.

He looked at the next pitch for strike three, and the Indians had to settle for tying the score. "He stinks," Paul muttered, and a couple of others agreed. But they said it softly so neither of their coaches would hear.

"Come on, guys. We'll get 'em next inning!" Derek said, pounding his catcher's mitt and leading the team back out onto the field.

Dave didn't walk anyone this time around, but he gave up a single—and then a double that went right over Gary's head when he didn't jump and try to get it. Several Indians groaned when that happened, but Mr. Jeter called out to them, clapping, "Come on, you guys! Hang together! Be a team!"

The first half of the second inning ended with the

Indians down 5–3 and a lot of unhappy players on the Indians' bench. Derek heard the whispers and muttering. He agreed with most of it. Okay, so Gary wasn't very good at baseball. There were plenty of kids who weren't, including a few on their own team. And even some kids with talent, like Dave, hadn't exactly played great so far.

But that wasn't the main problem. It was that Gary didn't even seem to be *trying*!

"Who cares?" Gary said, shrugging and smirking as he sat down to rest. "Win, lose, it's still the stupidest game on earth."

Derek knew it was really bad for a team to be divided against itself. So he went over to sit next to Gary. "Hey," he said, "can you just keep your feelings to yourself, Gary? At least until the game is over? The rest of us are trying to concentrate here."

Gary gave him a phony smile. "Sure, Derek. Hip, hip, hooray for us!" He clapped lazily, to show he was being sarcastic.

Derek turned away. Then he felt Gary pat him on the back. "Don't worry, Derek. I'll cool it. But only because you asked me so nicely."

Huh? "Th-thanks," Derek said uncertainly. Mason had struck out, and Dean was up. Derek went to grab his bat and get into the on-deck circle.

Suddenly laughter erupted on the bench. Looking at his teammates, Derek saw that they were laughing at *him*!

"What?" he asked. "What's going on?"

Jonathan pointed to Derek and said, "Dude, your back."

Derek frowned and reached behind him. There was a piece of paper stuck to his back! He ripped it off and read it out loud. "I JUST FARTED," it said. Glaring at Gary, Derek crumpled the paper up and threw it against the fence.

Gary just laughed. "Eeeuw!" he said, holding his nose like there was a bad smell. Eddie and Jonah laughed, as they always did at Gary's stupid jokes.

Derek had had enough. Dropping the bat, he walked back behind the fence and over to Gary, ready to make him apologize.

"Hey! Hey! Cut it out! NOW!" Mr. Jeter commanded. "Derek, I'm surprised at you."

"But, Dad—"

"You can call me 'Coach,'" said Mr. Jeter, "and you can take a seat as well. You too, Gary."

"Awww," said Gary, pretending to be unhappy. He sat down, and as soon as the coaches weren't looking, he raised his eyes skyward and mouthed the words "Thank you," smiling like a cat who had just eaten a tasty mouse.

"Dave!" Mr. Jeter barked, still looking sternly at Derek, who had plunked himself down on the bench in frustration and fury.

"Yessir?" Dave said, jumping up from the bench.

"You're catching next inning. Vijay!"

"Yes, Coach?"

"You're pitching."

"WHAT!" Derek blurted out.

"Dave, start warming him up, over there," said Mr. Jeter, pointing to a spot behind the bench where it was safe from foul balls.

"Me? Pitching?" Vijay said doubtfully.

"Just do the best you can," said Chase.

"All right, let's go!" the umpire called impatiently. "Play ball!"

"Eddie—you're batting for Derek, and playing left field," Mr. Jeter said, and the game resumed.

The Indians went down meekly in their half of the second, with Eddie pinch-hitting for Derek, who was now forced to watch from the bench as his replacement struck out to end the inning.

The game went south from there. Dave played fine at catcher, but Vijay had no feel for pitching at all. He walked a bunch of Cubs and gave up two home runs.

Mr. Jeter tried two other pitchers, but they didn't do any better. The Indians seemed to lose heart in the end, and wound up losing the game as well, by the gaping margin of 14–6.

Derek sat steaming through the whole game, which seemed endless to him. From time to time he glanced over at Gary, who was occupying the opposite end of the bench. Gary seemed pleased to be sitting this game out.

It was so *unfair*! Couldn't Derek's dad see that it was Gary who'd started it all?

After the game Mr. Jeter tried to buck up the team's spirits. "A lot of you did some good things that we've got to build upon. Coach Bradway and I are going to continue working with you individually as we go forward. You're all going to be better players by the end of this season, and hopefully that will translate into better results before too long."

He paused and cleared his throat. "Now, while I expect you all to make mistakes," he went on, "there's no room for negativity or taunting or fighting on the Indians. We're all on the *same team*, and I expect you to act that way. Anybody who doesn't will find a home on the bench, just like they did today."

He had to mean Gary and the kids who'd clowned around with him, thought Derek. But his dad was looking right at *him*. As if the fight had been Derek's fault!

"I have a question," Derek said, raising his hand.

"Derek?" said his dad.

"Why aren't you doing anything about kids who are fooling around?"

"Derek," said his father, "Coach Bradway and I will take care of any bad behavior going on, as you already experienced today. In addition, I don't want to hear any complaints from any of you about anyone else on the team. Let me say it again—we're a team. Remember that. That means we're on the *same side*, in case any of you need reminding."

He gave Derek another pointed look. "Understood?"

"Yes," said the team members—except Derek.

"Derek?" his dad said.

"Yes, I understand."

"All right. See you all next time."

Derek rode home in silence, while Vijay and Mr. Jeter discussed pitching. Mr. Jeter suggested that Vijay pitch to Derek between now and the next game, in case he ever had to pitch again.

Vijay begged to go back to the outfield, but Mr. Jeter only said, "We'll see. In the meantime I want you to be ready, just in case we need you."

Derek was perfectly willing to work with Vijay, but it was Gary he couldn't stop thinking about. Gary had succeeded in sabotaging the Indians, and in Derek's mind it was Gary who'd cost them the game.

He felt like screaming as he sat there. Gary's smile kept appearing in his mind. That kid loved riding the bench! As far as Gary was concerned, it beat playing a stupid game like baseball.

After they'd dropped Vijay off, Derek's dad said, "Derek, I can see you sulking back there. I'm sorry you're unhappy. But I have to say I was disappointed in your behavior today—no matter what anybody else did to provoke you. I expect better of you."

His words stung Derek to the quick. "Dad . . . ," he began, but then stopped, not knowing what to say.

Chapter Six

WRESTLING WITH THE MESS

How had this happened? Being coached by his dad had always been a big dream of Derek's. His dad wasn't doing a bad job of it either. Derek could see that he was teaching the other kids a lot of things, making them better hitters, fielders, and base runners. Chase was doing a good job too.

All of Derek's life, his dad had helped him get better at sports and games. From basketball to baseball, from chess to Scrabble—even guessing the prices on *The Price Is Right* on television—his dad had always challenged him to get better, to work harder, to concentrate more, to find solutions.

And now his dad was his coach for real! But so far it wasn't anything like Derek's dream. Right now his dad was mad at him and thought Derek was being a negative influence on the team.

But it *wasn't true*! Derek was trying his best, but Gary had a way of getting under his skin like nobody else. The worst part was, Gary was succeeding in sabotaging the team. They'd already lost their first game, and they seemed hopelessly divided against themselves.

"We won again!" Sharlee yelled, bursting into the house, with their mom right behind her. The smile on her face was so bright that Derek had to wince.

His mom was really happy too. "Sharlee hit two more homers, Jeter," she told her husband. "And she caught every ball at first base!"

"And Ciara's parents said she can sleep over on Saturday night!" Sharlee added, bubbling over with sheer joy. "Yaaay!"

Derek loved his sister like crazy, and that only made it worse that he felt so miserable. He knew he should be happy for her, but he just couldn't *feel* happy. He tried to smile, but he knew it wasn't much of one.

"We're 3–0, and we're never gonna lose!" Sharlee cooed. "Mommy, can I have ice cream now?"

"After dinner, Sharlee," said Mrs. Jeter, tousling her daughter's hair. "But you can have extra sprinkles."

"Yaay!"

Derek sighed. *Extra sprinkles.* What could he say?

• • •

An hour later the family sat together in their living room. Well, "together" might not have been the right word. Mr. Jeter was busy grading papers for his students at the university. Mrs. Jeter was doing extra work as an accountant. Sharlee was working on a puzzle, and Derek was watching the Tigers get slaughtered by the Indians. The *real* ones, on TV.

He didn't really care who won the game. His gaze veered to the window, where outside, the rain was falling heavily, a late afternoon thunderstorm.

If only it had rained like that during our game, he thought wistfully, *then we wouldn't have lost. . . .*

The phone rang, and Mrs. Jeter got up to answer it. "Hello? . . . Yes, he is. Just a moment. . . ." She took the receiver away from her ear and said, "Jeter, it's for you. Betty Parnell?"

Parnell? It had to be Gary's mom, thought Derek. But why was she calling his dad?

"Hello?" Mr. Jeter said into the phone. "Yes, hi, Mrs. Parnell. What can I do for you?"

There was a long silence, with Mr. Jeter nodding his head and frowning.

"Yes," he said now and then. "Mm-hmm. . . . I understand. . . ."

Was it possible? Could Gary really be quitting the team? Derek's heart was pounding, and he wished he could hear the other half of the conversation.

"Well, I—" Again his dad stopped talking, obviously having been interrupted. Derek could hear Mrs. Parnell across the room, yelling into the phone.

"You know what?" said Mr. Jeter. "Let me take this into the other room, where it's quieter, okay? Just hold on a moment. Thanks."

Putting the phone down, he blew out a breath, then said, "I'll be right back." Derek watched him disappear into the kitchen. "You can hang that extension up now, Dot," he called.

"Hmm," said Mrs. Jeter as she hung up the receiver. "I wonder what that's about. Your father seems to have upset somebody." She looked concerned but went back to her work.

"I'm . . . going up to study for my math test," Derek told her. "See you later."

"Okay, dear," his mom said without looking up.

Derek went out into the hallway. Then, instead of going up the stairs to his bedroom, he tiptoed farther down the hall, to the back door to the kitchen. There he stood, listening through the door as his dad dealt with Gary's mom over the phone extension.

"Mrs. Parnell," he was saying, "I agree with you in principle. And I agree that your son needs to get in better shape. But when he told me he had asthma, I—" Mr. Jeter broke off, interrupted again.

"That's right," he said. "That's what he told me. Are you

saying he doesn't? . . . I see. . . . Well, then I won't have to take *that* into consideration anymore. But there is still the matter of his attitude. . . ."

So his dad *did* realize what Gary was up to!

"Well, I can't have that sort of thing on my team. . . . Yes, I am the coach. And it's my job to make sure everyone on the team has a good experience. . . . Yes. . . . I'll tell you what. I'll make sure your son plays multiple innings next game, if you'll make sure he doesn't continue to disrupt the team. . . . I'm sure we can make this work for Gary as long as you and I are on the same page."

"Derek?"

Derek wheeled around, the blood rushing to his face. His mother stood there in the hallway, her hands on her hips.

"What do you think you're doing? You said you were going up to study."

"I . . . I got distracted."

"You had no intention of going up to study, did you?"

Derek looked at the floor, embarrassed. He couldn't lie to his mom.

She sighed, seeming to soften. "Come on away from there," she said, leading him into the little dining area. "So tell me," she said, sitting him down and pulling up a chair next to him. "What's this all about?"

"Gary's been ruining the team from the very beginning," he said. "He clowns around and makes fun of everything and everybody—especially me. And he gets me into trouble because I get mad about it! And some kids laugh at his jokes, and other kids laugh at *him,* because he's acting so dumb. And he stinks it up out there too! He doesn't even *care*, or want to get better! He just wants to sit on the bench. But obviously his mom wants him to play so that he gets in better shape! So the end result is, we're *doomed*! Last Place 'R' Us."

"Oh, Derek, it can't be as bad as all that," said his mom.

He gave her a look, not saying a word.

"That bad, huh? Wow. I'm so sorry, old man. And you've been looking forward to this for so long. . . ."

"You *see*?" he moaned. "And on top of everything else, Dad doesn't just blame Gary. He blames me! We *both* had to sit out most of the game, and our team lost! I'll bet if I'd been in there, we would've won!"

Mrs. Jeter sighed and nodded. "Possibly," she said. "But obviously your dad felt it was more important to be fair. I'm sure he wanted to nip this whole thing in the bud." She thought for a long moment, then continued.

"You know, Derek, it sure does sound like Gary's got a bad attitude. But at the same time, if the other kids aren't exactly welcoming him to the team, maybe he's just reacting to that. You know, people tend to like doing what they feel they're good at, or at least are getting better at. Maybe Gary would let you work with him on his game?"

Derek shook his head. "That'll never happen, Mom. Gary's not like other kids that way. He's . . . *different*."

"Really? Are you sure, Derek?" his mom asked. "I'll bet if you scratch the surface, you'll find you and Gary have more in common than you think."

As he lay in the dark, trying and failing to get to sleep, he kept hearing his mom's parting words, over and over again.

Could it possibly be true? Could he and Gary actually have something in common?

Derek sure hoped she was wrong, but in his experience, she hardly ever missed the mark.

Chapter Seven
GROWING PAINS

For game two, against the Yankees, Derek found himself playing the outfield—punishment, he assumed, for getting into it with Gary during the team's first game. Derek was totally bummed about being in center field, especially since Gary was starting the game in right.

"This stinks," Gary said with a sigh. "I'd much rather be anywhere else than here. Even worse is, your dad made my mom promise that I wouldn't get to have any fun at all around here."

Ah, so *that* was it! His dad *had* gotten through to Mrs. Parnell, and they were going to work together on Gary's behavior! So there would be no more clowning around on the bench, or sabotaging team spirit!

Well, that was a relief, for sure. Derek's confidence in his dad's wisdom returned to its normal, high level. "So, no more gags or stupid comments?"

Gary shook his head. "Depressing," he said.

"So . . . what are you going to do?"

Gary shrugged. "I guess I have no choice but to do my best, as painful as that may be. If I don't go along, my mom's not gonna let me go to math camp this summer."

Math camp? Derek rolled his eyes. How in the world did Derek's mom think he and Gary had anything in common?

At any rate Gary was going to give it his best. His best wasn't very good, of course, but at least he was going to try. That had to be an improvement.

"Play ball!" shouted the ump, and the first Yankees batter came to the plate.

The Indians started out with Dave on the mound for the second game in a row. And even though this time it was Miles catching instead of Derek, Dave fared no better. He was wild, in and out and up and down, walking three men in the first inning and two in the second. And when he did get it over, the Yankees hit it hard.

Worse, they hit it to Gary, not Derek. And Gary, even though he actually tried for once, still had trouble catching fly balls, or getting a good throw back in to the cutoff man.

The Yankees brought five runs across in those first two innings, while on their end the Indians scored three, behind Derek's and Dave's back-to-back homers in the first.

Still, the Indians were behind, and when they failed to score in their half of the second, Mr. Jeter took the ball from Dave.

Dave seemed downcast. It must have felt like he was getting fired from his job, thought Derek.

Chase was looking over at Dave like he wanted to console him. But Chase, like Mr. Jeter, had to be a coach first and a parent—or, in Chase's case, a substitute parent—second.

"Dean, take center field," Mr. Jeter continued. Turning and handing Derek the ball, he said, "You're pitching. Go out there and make Coach Bradway and me proud."

Derek nodded and set his jaw. "You got it, Dad—I mean, *Coach.*"

Derek didn't really like pitching. Maybe he would have if he'd thought he was better at it. But at least it beat the outfield, or catching, for that matter. You got plenty of action, without getting banged up and sore. Plus, the game was pretty much in your hands.

Derek knew that, like Dave, he had to put aside his own desires, for the good of the team. Okay, so he wasn't playing shortstop like he wanted to. But at least he wasn't on the bench!

Derek focused on what he'd learned in the past about pitching, from his dad and previous coaches. He tried to throw strikes, and he did pretty well.

He tried to keep the hitters off balance by changing speeds and the timing of his delivery. He succeeded at first, getting pop flies and ground balls. But after a while the Yankees started to figure him out.

In the fifth inning he gave up his first walk, to the lead-off batter. Then the cleanup hitter came up and doubled, hitting a slow pitch that hadn't fooled him. That scored a run to make it 6–3, Yankees.

The next batter hit a grounder to short, where Derek would have been playing if he'd had his wish. Instead it was Jonathan manning the position. He bobbled the ball, and it trickled to his left.

When the runner at second saw that, he took off for third. Jonathan recovered quickly and fired to third, but his throw was wild, and the runner came all the way home for the seventh run, while the hitter advanced to second!

The next batter hit a sharp liner to Jonathan, who ducked, sticking his glove out—and missing the ball. The eighth run scored, and Derek felt all the fight go out of him. Looking around, he saw that all his teammates had sagged after the two errors.

The coaches kept on shouting encouragement, and Derek rallied to strike out the next three hitters in a row, stopping the bleeding. But in spite of a sixth-inning comeback, the Indians lost their second game in a row, 8–5.

After the game Derek's dad told the team not to get down. "You boys played better today overall than last time," he said. "And I believe you'll play better in the next game than you did today. I see you all improving, every last one of you."

Derek looked around at his somber teammates. Even Gary seemed down, a change from the past, when he would have been exulting in the team's agony. Attitude-wise, at least, that was an improvement. Finally everyone on the team seemed to be on the same page.

Chase spoke up. "I know some of you made mistakes out there today," he said. "And I'm sure we'll be making our share of mistakes in the future. *Everyone* does. But if you keep working hard, keep the faith, and keep getting better every game, that'll translate into victories before too long. Are you with me?"

"Yeah," several team members said halfheartedly.

"Coach just said, 'ARE YOU WITH ME?'" Mr. Jeter echoed, sounding like he was still in the army.

That got them. The Indians all yelled, "YEAH!"

"That's better," Mr. Jeter said. "Now go home and think on all the things you did right today. We'll see you next time."

The team scattered. Mr. Jeter, Chase, Dave, Vijay, and Derek gathered all the gear and packed the team's duffel bags.

"Dave," said Chase, "take this bag over to the car, okay?"

"Sure thing," said Dave, hoisting the heavy bag and trudging off.

"Let's get these other bags," said Mr. Jeter. He and Vijay

each hoisted one and took off for the station wagon. "Bye, Chase," said Derek, about to follow them. "Tell Dave I felt bad about being put in to replace him today."

"Derek, sit down for a second."

Derek did as he was told. *What is this about?* he wondered.

Chase cleared his throat and ran his hands through his close-cropped hair. "I was just wondering how things were going for *you*."

"Me? Okay, I guess," Derek said flatly.

"I mean, you always seemed to be having so much fun out there playing ball. Big smile on your face and everything . . . But lately . . . well, let's just say your focus hasn't been the same. I was wondering if you noticed the same thing, and what might be throwing you off the track."

Derek shrugged. "I don't know," he said. "Maybe it's just that I haven't been playing short . . ."

"I know you want to be a shortstop, Derek, and your dad wants you to be too, of course. But do you want to know what I think? He's trying to get something across to you. Do you know what it is?"

"I'm . . . I guess I'm not sure."

"Don't worry. You'll figure it out for yourself," said Chase. "Just focus on how you can get back your love of playing the game. You'll get there, Derek. I know you will."

Derek got up to go. He hoisted the gear bag and started toward the car again. Why did everyone expect him to figure stuff out for himself? Why couldn't they just tell him what to do?

"Hang in there, Derek!" Chase called after him. "Just trust. Things will get better soon. Teams go through growing pains, you know—just like people."

Derek supposed Chase was right. But he sure hoped things turned around soon, before the season became a total bust.

Funny. . . . Both his mom and Chase seemed to be saying it was up to *him* to turn things around. But how could he do that? After all, he was only one player. Besides, he was just a kid! How was he supposed to figure everything out for himself?

Chapter Eight
LET'S MAKE A DEAL

"You know what I hate?"

Gary's question was in a whisper, because if Ms. Fein heard him, he'd get called out and given an *X* on his behavior chart. Gary had never had an *X* on his behavior chart—not because he didn't talk in class but because he was smart enough not to get *caught* at it.

Derek, however, even though he was smart in general, seemed to have a special hole in his brain when it came to getting caught talking in class. He had several *X*s in his chart, and Gary delighted in helping him get more of them, by baiting him into conversations that Derek couldn't resist.

Derek waited till Ms. Fein was busy shuffling some papers

on her desk, then whispered, "Okay, what do you hate?"

"I hate how all the guys on the team make fun of me."

Ms. Fein looked up from her papers, and Gary's mouth closed. His eyes had never left his worksheet, which he continued to scribble on even as he talked to Derek.

"You know," Derek murmured, watching Ms. Fein to make sure she wasn't looking, "if you learned to play better—or even acted like you cared—maybe they'd stop. I'll even talk to them about it, if you agree to come with me and my dad to the batting cages."

Gary snorted, which made Ms. Fein look up. "Do you have something to say, Derek?" she asked, a hand on her hip and her chin thrust forward.

"No, ma'am."

"Then please refrain from disturbing the rest of us."

"But—"

Derek stopped himself. He knew it was no use. Gary somehow had the supernatural ability to throw his voice like a ventriloquist, making it seem as if someone else were guilty, not him.

At least the teacher didn't open her chart and give Derek an *X*, he noted with relief. But was there anyone in the world more annoying than Gary Parnell? Not in Derek's world, there wasn't.

"Class? Attention please," the teacher said. Everyone put down their pencils and listened. "There's going to be a science test this coming Friday. It's going to count for ten percent of your grade this marking period, so I want you to study hard—and don't wait till the last minute either. You've got to go over units five, six, and seven."

There were moans and murmurs from some kids in the class. This really was going to be a big test. And that meant only one thing. . . .

"You know I'm beating you on this one," Gary told Derek. "As usual."

"That's what you *think* you know," Derek corrected him. He couldn't help getting into it with Gary. One thing they had in common was their sheer competitiveness.

Wait—that was *it*!

Derek remembered what his mom had said, that he and Gary had more in common than he thought. At the time, he couldn't see what, but now it seemed totally obvious!

And that gave him a brilliant idea. If Gary could bait Derek into doing things, Derek could do the same to him, by using Gary's own oversize competitive gene!

"Tell you what," he whispered to Gary. "If I beat you on this test, you have to come to the batting cages with me and my dad and learn how to hit."

Gary raised one curious eyebrow above the top of his glasses. "And if you lose?" he asked.

Derek shrugged. "Your call. You name it."

A sly grin appeared on Gary's face. He rubbed his hands together eagerly. "If you lose . . . you have to attend math camp with me the week after school ends!"

Math camp?

"All right, all right," Derek reluctantly agreed. "But tie goes to me."

No risk, no reward, he figured. And the potential reward was worth the risk. Not that he was going to let Gary beat him on this test. If he had to, Derek would stay up all night every night studying.

"It's a bet," Gary said out of the corner of his mouth.

"Yesss!"

"Derek Jeter!" Uh-oh. Ms. Fein had caught him red-handed. "You seem to have motormouth disease today. Maybe since you're so talkative, you'd like to talk to the principal?"

"No! I mean, no, Ms. Fein." The whole class was laughing at him now. Derek felt like melting into his chair.

"See me after class," said Ms. Fein. The bell rang. "As in, right now."

"Have fun, Jeter," said Gary, grinning as he gathered up his book. "I mean, motormouth! Ha!"

Gary's going to be sorry when I beat him on the test and he has to come to the batting cages, thought Derek.

"All right, young man. What is going on with you today that you feel it necessary to talk in class?"

"Ms. Fein, Gary kept talking to me, and I was—"

"Never mind what others did," she said, sounding just like Derek's mom and dad. "Let's talk about *you*. You already have five *X*s for talking. That's enough for me to put it on your report card, and that, I think you know, will get your parents involved."

"Oh, *please* don't do that, Ms. Fein," Derek begged. "I won't talk in class anymore, I promise! It's just that we were making a bet on who would get a better mark on the science test."

"Oh. I see," said Ms. Fein. "Well, then, since you're so interested in doing well on the test, you can do this extra science worksheet at home tonight. If you bring it in completed, I'll erase two of your *X*s, and you'll have done some extra studying for the test in the bargain!"

"Deal!" Derek said, happy and relieved. "You're the best, Ms. Fein!" He grabbed the worksheet, ran out of the class, and hurried to catch the school bus home.

Derek could feel his eyes crossing. He'd been studying for almost three whole hours, and it was nearly his bedtime. Vijay had called to see if he wanted to come over to the Hill and play ball, but Derek had turned him down, much to his pal's astonishment. It was the sort of thing that never happened—like lightning on a sunny day, or fish swimming in the toilet.

"Derek?" It was his dad, popping his head into Derek's room. "How's it going?" His dad's tone was warm and friendly, and he was smiling.

"Good," Derek said, stifling a yawn.

"You've been at it all evening, I notice. Big test?"

"You have no idea how big."

"Uh-huh. Well, I'm glad to see you working so hard and taking your schoolwork seriously. I want you to know how proud I am of that."

"Thanks," Derek said, yawning for real this time.

"Sure you don't want to stop now and get some sleep?"

Derek shook his head. "I've still got this extra worksheet I volunteered to do."

"*Volunteered? For extra work?*"

"Uh-huh."

"Well, good for you! That's great. I'm proud of you, like I said. And I'm also proud of how hard you're trying out there on the ball field. You've played very well, no matter where I've put you. You've been steady and consistent at the plate. No errors at all so far. And no *complaining* anymore about your teammates. I noticed that, too. So . . . good going."

"Thanks, Dad."

Mr. Jeter said, "I notice you've been checking out your contract too." The contract was sitting right on Derek's desk. He'd checked it to see what the penalty was for talking too much in class.

"Hey, Dad?"

"Yes?"

"What about Dave? Are you going to let him pitch again next game? I know he wants to."

"Derek, I've got to give other kids a chance on the

mound. And that's all I'm going to say about it," he added when Derek looked like he wanted to object. "Let's stay focused on the positives, okay?"

"Uh-huh. I'd better get back to work, though," Derek told his dad. "Got to do that worksheet."

"All right. But don't stay up too late."

"I won't."

It took Derek another half hour to do a worksheet that should have taken only ten minutes. But he couldn't keep his mind from drifting, as tired as he was.

He ran over the Indians' last game in his mind—and all the ones before that. All the mistakes, all the "what ifs." None of it changed a thing. Their record was a disaster so far, and if things didn't turn around right away, the whole season would become an exercise in frustration.

Now if only he could beat Gary on this test and get him down to the batting cages, where Derek and his dad could both work on Gary's game—*and* his attitude!

Chapter Nine
SMELLS LIKE TEAM SPIRIT

"I know I could do it, if I could only get another shot," Dave said glumly.

He, Derek, and Vijay, along with half a dozen other kids from Mount Royal Townhouses, were playing ball on "Derek Jeter's Hill," the grassy slope where the kids always gathered after school.

"I don't know why you even want to pitch," Vijay said as he took the ball for his turn on the mound. "I hate pitching. I don't know why Coach made me do it that time."

"You'd like it if you were better at it," Dave said.

"What do you mean? I stink at it!"

"See? That's what I'm saying!" said Dave. "You're proving my point."

Turning to Derek, who had on the team's catcher's gear, Dave said, "I wish your dad would give me another chance. Do you think he ever will?"

Derek shrugged. "I have no idea."

"Couldn't you ask him for me? I'll bet he'd listen to you."

"You'd lose that bet. My dad makes up his own mind about things. And he's been pretty clear about me not interfering with his coaching decisions."

Intervening on Dave's behalf was out of the realm of possibility. He hadn't told Dave that he'd already asked once, and been shut right down.

"Hey, you guys!" their friend Josh yelled from the outfield. "How 'bout it? We're waiting!"

"Hang on one second!" Derek shouted back. "I'm sure he'll give you another shot eventually," he assured Dave, although he was really far from sure.

Derek could see that what he'd said didn't make Dave any happier.

"The thing is, I want to make sure I come through if I *do* get another chance," Dave said. "Do you think you could help me figure out what I'm doing wrong?"

Derek thought of his mom's words: "How can you yourself make sure your team plays up to its potential?"

"Sure," he said. "How about if we stay around for half an hour after the other kids go home? We could work on your delivery and your grip—you know, just the two of us?"

Dave's face lit up with hope. "Really? Sounds perfect!"

"Will that be okay with Chase, though?"

Dave's driver and guardian was always nearby, hanging out by the fancy Mercedes that was almost as big as a limo. He kept a close eye on all of Dave's social activities.

"I'll ask him," Dave said. "But, hey, he's our coach too. How can he say no?"

Sure enough, Chase agreed to an extra half hour of play before driving Dave home to do his homework and have supper.

Derek asked Vijay to stop at the Jeter house and let his parents know he'd be a little late getting home.

"If they say no, come back and tell me," he said.

"Okay, Chief!"

"Chief?"

"Well, I would call you 'Coach,' because now you are going to coach Dave, but we already have two coaches, so it would be too confusing."

"Whatever," Derek said, laughing. Vijay never failed to crack him up. Turning to Dave and handing him the ball, he said, "Pitch to me."

Dave went out to the tree root that served as the mound. He started throwing to Derek, who was still wearing the catching gear and mitt. Good thing too, because Dave's fastballs hurt his palm when they hit the pocket of his mitt. "Ouch!" he said. "Man, you've got some pop!"

"I know! But it doesn't do me any good up there, does

it? I can't get it over half the time, and the other half, they clobber it."

"Well, let's tackle one thing at a time. First of all, let's get it over the plate. I can see that you're not finishing."

"Huh?"

"Your motion. You've got to let go of the ball when your hand is pointed right at the target." Derek squatted down and made a target with his mitt. "Try it."

Dave did—and the ball hit right in the mitt. Derek didn't even have to move his glove.

"Wow! That works!" Dave exulted.

"Now do it ten more times."

Dave tried, and had trouble repeating the motion.

"Don't get down about it," Derek advised him. "You've got to make it a habit. Now on the follow-through let your arm keep going, and try to end up with your feet square to home plate, so that you can field the ball if it comes to you."

They worked on one thing and another, with Dave making adjustments as he went. Then Derek said, "We've got only about ten minutes left. So let's work on giving you a changeup."

"A *what*?"

Sometimes Derek had to remind himself that a year ago, when they'd first met, Dave had never played a game of baseball, or even watched it much on TV.

Dave's sport was golf. In fact, his dream of being a

professional golf champion was a lot like Derek's dream of being starting shortstop for the New York Yankees. Having dreams in common was what had made them best friends.

"A *changeup*. A slow pitch, to throw the hitters off. They're watching your fastball on every pitch, right? Timing it, so that when you finally get it over, they're ready to roll. But if you throw them a changeup every few pitches, they'll swing too early and either miss it or make bad contact."

"Huh. Sounds interesting. So how do I do it? Just throw more slowly?"

"It's more complicated than that."

Remembering how his own dad had taught him, Derek showed Dave how to hold the baseball deep in his hand—unlike with the fastball, which is thrown using the fingertips.

"See? Holding it tighter is what makes the ball slow down. But you throw it with the same motion as your fastball, which means the hitter can't tell the pitches apart!"

"Cool!" Dave said. "Let's try it."

They tried a few dozen, with occasional success, before Chase honked the horn.

"We'll keep at it," Derek told him. "Got to form those habits."

"Thanks! I feel much better about things. At least about getting better at pitching. Of course, it won't mean anything if I never get to pitch again. . . ."

"Don't get down, Dave. Things will turn around. You never know when you're going to get your shot. You just have to be ready when it happens."

Dave smiled and nodded. "Thanks again—*Chief*," he said, and took off for the car.

Derek shook his head as he watched his friend go. Man, it was amazing how much his dad had taught him over the last few years. Derek had learned it so well that now he was even able to pass it along to his teammates.

"I can't believe you beat me by one measly point!"

Gary held the metal bat like it was dirty toilet paper, and he looked like he was about to vomit. "It must have been a mistake—a clerical error, for sure! There's no other rational explanation."

"Maybe I just studied harder than you," Derek said, not bothering to suppress his grin. "Or maybe I'm just a *little* smarter."

"Give me a break," said Gary, rolling his eyes.

Okay, so maybe Derek wasn't smarter than Gary. But one thing was sure—he was smarter than Gary *thought* he was! And he'd *outsmarted* Gary this time, beating him on the science test by getting a 99 over Gary's 98, and forcing Gary to make good on his bet.

Here came Mr. Jeter now, having paid in advance for their batting cage session. "You boys ready?"

"You bet!" said Derek.

"Errghh," said Gary in a tone of sheer dread.

"First of all," said Mr. Jeter, opening the cage door to let them in, "that's not how you hold a bat, Gary. But you know that, right?"

Gary sighed. "Okay, how's this?" He adjusted his hands to hold the bat the way he did during a game.

"Well, that's *closer*," said Mr. Jeter, "but your hands shouldn't be apart like that. Slide your right hand down a couple of inches."

"Like *this*?"

"That's it. Relax your left hand, though. It doesn't have to be twisted up like that. Now let's see how you stand in the box."

"I don't like standing in boxes," Gary quipped. "I'm claustrophobic."

"I like a man with a sense of humor," said Mr. Jeter, clapping Gary on the back.

Derek noticed that his dad didn't get mad at Gary for wisecracking, the way he would have if Derek had tried it. Instead he managed to disarm Gary's resistance with a mix of humor and focus.

"You must be really steamed at my mom, huh?" Gary said, trying anything that might waste more of their precious half hour, without him having to actually swing a bat.

"Not at all," said Derek's dad. "In fact I admire her. She's a smart lady who's being the best mom she knows how to be."

That caught Gary off guard. "Oh," he said. "Look, let's be honest. There's no point in this fruitless exercise. I'm just too uncoordinated to hit a baseball. And that's a proven fact."

"Not at all," Derek's dad said again. "You've got power potential, and if you'll just step a little closer to the plate, I'll prove it."

Gary was out of excuses. Derek's dad had outmaneuvered him at his own game, and Gary was forced to stand in the box and take some swings.

Mr. Jeter showed him how to be ready on time and hit the ball hard. He taught Gary to keep his bat level through the hitting zone and stay balanced through the swing.

It was more or less the same way he'd taught Derek how to hit over the years, except compressed into about twenty minutes' time.

Step by step Mr. Jeter worked with Gary, as patient as a stone, ignoring sighs and protests, gently nudging him into the right stance, with the right grip, and helping him swing with his body parts working together instead of at odds.

By the end of their half hour, Gary was hitting line drives on pitches that weren't much slower than the ones he'd be facing the next day.

Derek had to smile, shaking his head. It was absolutely amazing that in such a short time Gary looked like a completely different hitter—one who could actually, conceivably, possibly help the team win!

"Well, I have to admit, your dad's pretty smart," said Gary as they were putting the bats back into the racks before leaving. Mr. Jeter was up front again, talking with the owner about one of the machines that was malfunctioning.

Derek laughed. "Funny, I was just thinking the same thing."

His dad was an amazing coach, in addition to being an amazing dad. Look at how hard he'd worked with every kid on the team, making them better, never giving up on them.

"No wonder you're not half-bad in science and math," Gary said. "But you could still get better. Look at me and hitting."

"I can't argue with that."

"Now, if you were really, *really* smart, you'd come with me to math camp anyway. Just for fun!"

Derek couldn't believe his ears. "Fun?"

"You'd be surprised. It's a total blast."

"Seriously?"

"Hey, if I can be surprised about hitting, you can be surprised about math."

"Thanks, but I don't think so," Derek said, smiling.

"Double or nothing next test?"

"It's tempting . . . but no. I like math fine, but math camp might be a step too far for me. Anyway, thanks for showing up today. I hope you're glad you came."

"I actually am, amazingly. Although, I have my doubts about whether it will translate into competition. Sports have a way of stressing me out, you know? Especially baseball. It's so *lame*."

Derek shook his head. Gary was a hard case, no doubt about it.

Still, Derek had to agree with Gary about his success in the batting cage. Anyone but a fool would have doubts about whether it would translate into better hitting in actual games.

Chapter Ten

WELCOME TO THE CELLAR

"That's it—just like that. Now do it again, three more times."

Derek flipped the ball back to Dave, who gripped it deep in his palm, using three fingers to hold it instead of two.

"Nasty!" Derek said as Dave's newly honed changeup floated into his mitt. "And you're getting it over more often too. Now back to the fastball."

Dave gripped the ball with just two fingers and his thumb, holding the ball mostly with his fingertips, and let fly.

Pop! "Ow!" Derek said, shaking his glove hand. "That hurt!"

Dave flashed a smile, and Derek felt good that he'd raised his friend's spirits, as well as his game. "Keep it up, and you're going to be our staff ace before you know it."

Derek felt pleased with himself. He was doing what he could to make his team and its players better—with Gary, and now with Dave.

"Thanks, Derek," said Dave as they wrapped up their practice session on the Hill. "And thanks for working with me. It really made a difference, even if I don't get to pitch again."

"You will. Don't worry," said Derek. "I'm going to tell my dad how well you're doing."

"Cool!"

Derek wished he hadn't said that. It made Dave feel better, but Derek wasn't at all sure his dad would be receptive to suggestions about where to put his players.

Up till now Derek's pleas had not been successful. But the team was 0–2 and about to face the Twins, who were 2–0. If the Indians didn't turn their fortunes around soon, it would be too late to save their season, no matter who played where.

Derek stood at shortstop, pounding his glove as he waited for the bottom of the first to start. It was a relief to be out here, even though he'd struck out in the top of the first with a man on base.

He knew what he'd done wrong. He'd let his concentration wander, thinking too much about hitting a home run and getting the Indians on the board, instead of just seeing the pitch and putting good wood on it. He would not make that same mistake next time up, he promised himself.

For now, though, the main thing was to keep his focus on each and every pitch and to do his job at shortstop, so that his dad had no reason to reconsider Derek's fielding position.

Dave was at third, looking longingly at the mound, where Jonathan was ready to pitch instead of him. Dave gave Derek a glance, and Derek nodded back, as if to say, *Never mind. Let's just win one. Then we'll think about the rest.*

Jonathan's first pitch got clobbered, but Vijay played it well and threw it back in to keep it to a single. On the next pitch, though, the runner took off, trying to steal second. Paul, who was catching, fired a strike to Derek, who was covering the base, and Derek tagged the runner just in time!

Derek raised his glove to show the ump he still had the ball, but somehow the ump called the runner safe!

Derek moaned and threw his hands into the air—but quickly recovered his senses, knowing it was disrespectful to protest the umpires' calls too much. Disrespect was not acceptable at all, and it even said so in his contract.

So now the Twins had a runner on second. Two ground balls followed, one to Derek and one to Tito at first. The runner advanced to third on the first out, and scored on the second, to give the Twins the lead.

The cleanup hitter was next. He hit a long fly ball to right, where Gary was playing. Gary had it lined up perfectly but still managed to miss the ball, after losing it in the sun—or just plain ducking, trying not to get hurt.

Whichever, it resulted in the ball's dropping. The next hitter scored two on an inside-the-park home run to make it 3–0, Twins.

Things started looking up after that. The Indians got out of the inning without any further trouble, and got a run in the top of the second when Gary, of all people, hit a sharp single to right to score Vijay, who'd doubled in front of him.

Derek couldn't help feeling hopeful. Gary's hit had been no accident, he knew, but rather had been the result of his time in the cages with Derek's dad. His swing looked miles better than before, and Derek only wished he'd suggested to Gary that they spend some time on fielding practice too. Not that Gary would have agreed to it, of course. But still . . .

Jonathan got through the second and third innings okay. Then the Indians came back to tie the game, with Derek turning a single into a triple when the outfielder bobbled the ball and then threw wide to second, and scoring on the next pitch when Dave hit a long, screaming line drive of a home run. Gary had another single that inning but was stranded on base when Mason struck out to end the inning.

It was in the fourth inning that things fell apart for the Indians. Jonathan seemed to tire, or maybe he just lost his rhythm. Either way, he couldn't find the strike zone. He walked four out of five hitters, letting in two runs, and Derek's dad had to replace him.

Derek thought for a second he was going to motion for

Dave to take over. But Mr. Jeter called on Paul instead, inserting Miles at catcher and sitting Jonathan down.

Paul had a good arm, but he had never pitched in a game, and had only thrown off a mound in practice a few times. Clearly Mr. Jeter, having tried everyone else he could think of, was just looking to catch lightning in a bottle. But Paul's inexperience showed when he gave up a bases-clearing double to his first hitter, before getting it together and registering three straight outs.

At 8–3 the game was no longer close. Derek hit a two-run homer in the sixth, but 8–5 was as close as they came. The game ended with the bases loaded and Tito striking out on a pitch over his head.

Derek felt like he'd been crushed. The team had done better than in their first two games, but what good was better if it only added up to another loss?

The Indians were 0–3 now, and only a miracle could save them from ending up a losing team.

Derek knew how hard his dad and Chase had worked to make the team better. But he couldn't help wondering when all of that work would start showing up in the form of victories.

Mr. Jeter and Chase tried their best to pick the team up afterward, but it was a downcast group of Indians who straggled away from the field, losers again in spite of everything.

Even Vijay seemed unusually down. "Well, we did score

five runs," he offered. "That makes three games in a row where we've scored at least that many."

Derek gave him a doubtful look. "Doesn't matter how many you score if the other team scores more," he said.

His dad gave him a glance in the rearview mirror. "Vij is right, Derek," he said. "The team's been hitting pretty well—better each game, in fact. And everybody's attitude is better too. At least it was until we lost today. So there's a lot to build on. We just have to find us someone who can pitch."

He gave Derek another look in the mirror. "I was thinking you might start practicing pitching for the next game—"

"Dad," Derek protested. "You know I don't want to pitch! I want to play short!"

"And you did very well today, I thought," said his dad. "Don't worry. I'm going to keep you out there, at least for part of the game. But I need to find pitchers."

"Don't look at me!" Vijay said. "I tried it already once, and it was a disaster."

"You weren't too bad," Mr. Jeter assured him. "But there's got to be somebody we can count on to hold the other team down while we build a lead. Someone who can start the games and stay in there until we're ahead by a few." Another glance at Derek. "Then I can bring you in to close the games."

Derek had never thought of himself as a closer, or even as a pitcher. But he was willing to do anything at this point to help the team win. And he had the perfect solution to the problem too, if only his dad would listen!

"Dad?" he said after they'd dropped Vijay off. "I think you should give Dave another shot at pitching."

"Dave?" Mr. Jeter repeated. "He's already had two shots, and they didn't work out very well, I'm afraid. You know how much I like Dave, Derek, but—"

"But he's much better!" Derek broke in. "You should see. Just try him in the next game! I've been—"

Mr. Jeter cut him off. "Derek, I think we've had this conversation before. You let me be the coach, and just keep working on your own game. You were good out there today, but that doesn't mean you can't be better. Take care of your own business, and let me and Chase take care of ours. How about helping Gary with his fielding, if you want to make things better?"

Now he'd gone and annoyed his dad again, Derek realized. But he also knew that Dave, with his new changeup and better accuracy, could be the answer to the team's pitching woes.

He knew his dad was right about letting the coaches coach, but he was desperate to show his father how much better Dave had gotten with his help.

The problem was, how was he ever going to get his dad to notice?

Chapter Eleven

STUCK TOGETHER

"Class, come to order," said Ms. Fein, clapping her hands to get her students' attention. When they'd calmed down, she said, "I'm going to assign a final work project in math for the year. You'll have two weeks to turn it in, and it will count for twenty percent of your grade. I want five pages of explanation, along with charts, illustrations, whatever you can come up with to help us understand your thesis. It should have to do with any topic we've dealt with this year in school. That would include fractions, percentages, long division, etc. I leave the rest up to you. Be creative."

Groans went up from several kids in class who obviously preferred multiple-choice tests to creative math projects. And no wonder, thought Derek. Projects were a whole lot more *work*. That was obviously why it was going to count for so much of their grade.

Derek liked math. It was pretty much his favorite subject, because he was naturally good at it. But he liked it a whole lot less after Ms. Fein added, "I'm going to assign you each a partner for this project. Let's start with Vijay. You and Christine pair up. Dave, you and Teresa. Josh, you and Monica. Derek, you and . . . Gary."

Yeesh. Stuck with him *again!* Derek thought, wincing. Looking over at Gary, he saw that his new partner was just as unhappy.

"I will expect a proposed topic from each team by tomorrow," their teacher concluded. "You can start discussing it right now, since we have only five more minutes in the period. But softly!" she added when the class burst into an instant uproar. "This is math class, not the debate team!"

Gary turned to Derek, who occupied the desk right next to him, which was probably why the teacher had paired them up. "I have a great idea."

"Oh, goodie," said Derek without enthusiasm.

"Get this. We develop an algorithm to predict chess moves!"

"A what?"

"An algo— Oh, never mind. If you don't even know what one is, you sure aren't going to be any help coming up with one. Okay, Mr. Know-It-All, let's hear *your* great ideas."

"Um . . ." Derek thought for a moment. "I've got one! How about we do a project on baseball statistics!"

Gary rolled his eyes and pretended to choke himself. "That," he finally said, "is the worst idea I have ever heard in my entire life. Talk about two weeks of torture!"

"How can you say that?" Derek asked. "Sports has so much math in it—especially baseball!"

"Yeah, right," Gary said, and snorted.

"I'm telling you, it's even more mathified than chess."

"No way."

"Yes way!" Derek insisted. "Check this out. There's batting averages, slugging percentages, ERAs, OBPs, games behind—and that's just for starters!"

Gary's eyes widened as Derek laid out what his mom, the accountant, had shown him a couple of years earlier, when he and his parents had been putting together his contract. His mom and dad had been trying to show him why school was important, even if you wanted to become a professional ballplayer.

"You know," said Gary when Derek had finished, "I hate to admit this, but for once in your life, you've actually got a point. Baseball's got a lot more math in it than I gave it credit for—*almost* enough for me to have a *teensy-weensy* bit of respect for it. Too bad it's such a dumb game otherwise. But at least now it won't be a complete waste of my time."

"You mean you'll do it?" Derek asked.

"Mmmm. . . . Okay, why not?" said Gary with a shrug.

"We'll have to spend a lot of time working out everyone's average on our team, of course. And there'll have to be charts, spreadsheets . . ."

"I can do that part," said Derek excitedly. "You can look up the averages of the major-league Indians and see how the two match up!"

"Sounds like a plan," Gary said. "And what's our thesis?"

Derek grinned. "That's easy—that we're better than they are, at least for our age!"

"You've got to be kidding me!" Gary said, surprised. "We stink. We haven't even won one stupid game yet."

"Hey, have you checked out the real Indians this season?" Derek asked with a grin. "They're in last place by a lot! We might wind up being better, especially if we start winning games."

"Hah! Like that'll ever happen," said Gary as the bell rang. "I might be hitting the ball better now, but I'll *never* figure out how to operate a baseball glove. It's such a stupid piece of equipment, it's ridiculous. Deformed, even. All you have to do is look at it to see that." He shook his head. "Well, partner, see you in study period tomorrow."

"I've got to admit," Derek said as the two sat together at a long table in the cafeteria for their first work session, "I'm amazed you agreed to do this project on baseball stats."

"Yeah, well," Gary said with a shrug. "I figure it this way. You and I are the two best math brains in the class."

"Not counting Vijay."

"Eehhhhh . . . ," Gary said, unimpressed, holding one hand palm-down and shaking it, to indicate that he thought Vijay's math chops were just so-so.

"But to go along with a project on baseball . . . ," Derek said. "That's surprising to me."

Gary clucked his tongue and shook his head dismissively. "It almost doesn't matter what we do it on, so long as we beat the pants off all those other teams."

Derek had to laugh. Gary was the only kid he'd ever met who was as competitive as he was! His mom had been right all along. They *did* have something in common, something huge.

"And trust me, Jeter, we will be victorious—*if* you take on your half of the responsibility."

"Huh? What do you mean by that?" Derek asked, taking offense.

Gary put a hand on one hip and looked over at the chart Derek had been trying without success to put together for the past half hour. "I mean *that*. That *mess* you've got there. What exactly is that supposed to *be*, anyway?"

"It's our team's batting averages, game to game. I tried putting it in crosswise, but I think I did it wrong."

"You *did* do it wrong, *of course*," said Gary, as obnoxious as ever.

"Well, I don't really get how it's supposed to look. It's not my fault. We haven't really done graphs."

"What are you talking about? We did them back in November, remember?"

"I was sick with chicken pox those two weeks, *remember*?" Derek shot back smartly.

Gary sighed as if he were carrying a sack of heavy stones. "I can tell I'm going to have to get this team across the finish line by myself. Here, let me show you how it's done."

Derek wanted to argue, but he wanted even more to let Gary make the chart for him. Five minutes later it was done, and perfectly.

"Thanks, Gary," said Derek sincerely. "I appreciate the help. Now if you could just take five more minutes to explain it to me, so I can understand it."

"Why should I waste five precious minutes of my life to teach you what you should have learned yourself months ago?"

"Just because . . . because we're friends."

"Friends?" Gary could not have looked more stunned.

Derek suddenly had a great idea. He couldn't understand why it hadn't occurred to him before.

"And because we're friends now, if you help me out and explain graphs to me so I can ace that part of the math final, I'll help you with your fielding!"

"Huh?"

"Your *fielding*, man! Now that you can hit, it's the only thing keeping you from being a decent ballplayer. Just think, you might even shut those kids up who've been making fun of you all this time! And *we* might just start winning some ball games."

"In your dreams."

"Come on!" Derek said, getting excited about the idea of coaching Gary and improving his game. "All you have to do is show up at the Hill after school tomorrow. I'll get Vijay and Dave out there to help us too. It'll take only an hour or so. Come on, trust me. I can help you! I mean, it's only fair, after how you're about to help me."

"I *am*? Who says I am?" But then he grinned, showing Derek he was only joking. "Okay, okay, I'll help you out, Jeter. But forget about paying me back like that. *Extra time playing sports?* It's bad enough I already have to show up for the games. Besides, there are always a ton of kids over there at the Hill. I don't need to get made fun of any more than I already have been."

"That's just it! Once *I* get through with you, you won't be getting made fun of anymore, because you'll be as good with a glove as any of them!"

Gary gave him a doubtful look.

"Well . . . at least you won't be embarrassing," Derek corrected himself.

Gary seemed to be about to relent. "Well . . . I don't know . . ."

"Besides, you're already *hitting* the ball okay, thanks to my dad. Believe me, I may not know how to draw a chart, but I know stuff about fielding that'll make you better, and quick."

Gary sighed again, as if the weight of the whole world were on his shoulders. "Oh, okay," he said, sounding completely defeated. "But just this one time, and for one hour max."

"Done!" Derek said, clapping his hands in triumph. "We can do it right after school tomorrow—before Vijay, Dave, and the rest of the kids even get there. That way you won't have to get made fun of."

"Good idea."

Seeing the relieved look on Gary's face, Derek realized just how much all the teasing must have gotten to him. Beneath his hardened exterior, Gary actually had *feelings*, just like anybody else!

Unbelievable, but true.

"And I *promise* I'm going to work hard on this project next session," Derek said. Smiling, he added, "That is, if *you'll* get a better attitude about sports."

Gary gave him a sickly smile in return. "You first, smarty-pants."

Derek couldn't get the grin off his face as he headed to the Hill the next day after school. He wasn't technically allowed to play ball until he'd done that day's homework, but this one time he had talked his dad into letting him go, saying that coaching Gary in fielding was part of their project about baseball stats and math.

When Mr. Jeter saw what Derek was trying to do, he smiled and gave his permission, provided Derek came right back home afterward and did his homework.

Now for the hard part. Teaching Gary to field was going to be a challenge. He had no natural instincts for the game, no athleticism, and no interest in improving. But Derek had lured him by promising he could stop the others from teasing him. Now Derek had to come through.

Yikes.

Gary was there, right on time. "Okay, let's get this torture session over with so I can go home and have fun doing homework." He checked his watch. "One hour. No, wait. . . . Fifty-nine minutes left. Go!"

Derek went into a momentary panic. Here he was, face-to-face with the biggest challenge he could think of. His mind actually went totally blank for a moment.

Then he saw Gary's baseball mitt.

"That thing looks like it's never been worn!" he said, taking it from Gary and examining it. He put it on his hand and tried to clamp it shut—unsuccessfully.

"It's as hard as a rock!" he said. "No wonder you can't catch anything with it."

"Huh? I thought that was how it was *supposed* to be."

"No!"

"But all the other gloves in the store were the same way."

"Because they've never been used! Gary, didn't anyone ever tell you you have to break a glove in?"

"Break it *what*?"

"Oh boy," Derek said, realizing just how much Gary had to learn about baseball. "Look, feel *my* glove. Go ahead, try it on."

Gary did. "Ooohhh. Wow, this thing is just about worn to shreds. It feels like a glove."

"It *is* a glove, for goodness' sake! Don't you get it? You've got to stomp on your glove, have your mom run over it with the car, rub it down with saddle soap or grease, kick it around!"

"Hey, this glove cost thirty dollars!"

"Gary, it's no good if you don't break it in somehow, and it never will be. Here, let's try playing catch, except you wear my glove."

He positioned Gary about fifty feet away so that they could toss the ball back and forth. Right away Derek noticed an improvement in Gary's ability to get and keep the ball in his mitt.

"Two hands!" Derek reminded him when a ball or two dropped from Gary's grasp. "Catch it in the webbing, not in the pocket. That's it! Next time clamp it shut—with both hands."

Little by little Gary seemed to get more comfortable catching the ball. And with that comfort, his fear of the baseball hitting him in the face seemed to lessen.

"This is actually sort of cool," Gary had to admit after about fifteen minutes. "I feel like I almost, kind of, sort of know what I'm doing."

"I'm telling you, man, the better you get at baseball, the more you're going to love it."

"Gag me with a spoon," said Gary, making a nice one-handed grab of a ball Derek had thrown too high.

"Nice one!"

"Thanks!" Gary said, tossing it back wildly. "Ha! You missed it!"

"This glove's pretty impossible," Derek admitted. "You're going to go home and mess with it, right?"

"I like the part about my mom running it over with the car," Gary said with a grin. "Yaaaaa! Take that, stupid baseball!"

Derek laughed, and then proceeded to show Gary some of the finer points of fielding—how to shield his eyes from the sun with his mitt, how to run back on a ball over his head, how to know where to throw it after he caught it when there were men on base.

Derek might have been an infielder, but his dad had trained him well, putting him in different positions early in the season, so that he knew a little about outfielding from actual experience. All of that helped Derek now as he tried to help Gary with his game.

Had his dad seen all this coming? Was *that* why he'd insisted that Derek play those other positions? Derek wouldn't have been surprised. His dad sometimes seemed to have eyes in the back of his head, and a periscope into the future, too.

Vijay and Dave arrived, along with a couple of other kids. "Nice catching!" Vijay exulted when he saw how much improved Gary's glove work was.

"Amazing!" Dave agreed. "Hey, man, you do that in the game, and we're gonna be a better team!"

After throwing it around for a while, Gary remembered to check his watch. "Hour's up!" he announced. "Thank goodness that's over."

Derek felt hurt. Even after their session Gary was still putting down sports. But then, when he and Gary were exchanging gloves, he saw from Gary's wristwatch what time it actually *was*. Gary had been playing for an hour and a half, without even realizing it!

"Hey, time flies when you're having fun," Derek said with a twinkle in his eye.

"Very funny," said Gary.

"You know what?" Derek asked. "I know you think we make each other better in school by competing. But I think we do even better when we *cooperate* and act like we're on the same team."

"Hmm. You might actually have something there, Jeter. Oh, by the way . . ."

Gary reached into his back pocket and pulled out a folded piece of paper. "Here are *your* statistics for the season so far, complete with the graphs that were supposed to be *your* job to make."

"Thanks!" Derek said, unfolding the paper and looking at his stats come to life in charts and graphs, perfectly done in easy-to-decipher colors. "You're going to do this up bigger, right?"

"*And* I've got the charts and graphs for every member of our team, *and* for the team as a whole, *and* for the major-league Indians, too." Gary stuck his chin out proudly. "*And* I've already designed a system to keep it up to date."

"Wow!" Derek said. "Okay, I admit it. You *are* smarter than me."

"Smarter than *I*, not *me*."

"Whatever. I'm just glad we're on the same team."

Frankly, Derek was totally floored. Gary had outdone himself, and Derek was sure to profit from it. On top of everything else, it seemed like Gary had finally found a way to get excited about baseball!

Now, if the work they'd done on Gary's fielding translated into better play on the field, things might actually turn around for the Indians!

Chapter Twelve

TURNAROUND

The Indians were a nervous-looking bunch before their fourth game of the season. Everyone knew what today's game meant. If they lost and went to 0–4, there was not much chance of ever digging out of that hole.

For some team members that might not have been a big deal. Eddie, Jonah, and Gary had probably never imagined winning a championship. They hadn't been much into the spirit to begin with, and Gary's antics hadn't helped. By now they'd probably given up on the rest of the season.

But for the rest of the kids, being 0–3 was a thorn in their sides. Either it was going to be removed with a win today, or it was going to be stuck there for the rest of the season. Even the usually sunny and optimistic Vijay seemed tense and anxious.

The coaches did their best to get the players into the right frame of mind. But feeling good about their prospects was tough for the players, especially since they were going up against the first-place, undefeated Giants today. None of the Giants' games had even been close. Their hitters were being talked about all over the league.

Derek wished his dad would change his mind and put Dave back in at pitcher. Derek had been working with him for a week and a half now, and Dave had improved a lot. His changeup looked just like his fastball, and Derek felt sure it could fool even the best hitters. Dave's fastball had better location now, and he had learned how to follow through so that he ended up in a good fielding position.

Derek was tempted to beg his dad to make a switch, but he knew it wasn't his place and that his dad wouldn't like it. So he kept silent as Jonathan warmed up.

Jonathan wasn't bad on the mound, but he had neither Dave's arm strength nor his control. Jonathan didn't have a changeup, either. Against the Giants' hitters, that did not bode well for success today.

"Hey, team!" came a familiar voice from behind Derek. Turning around, he saw Gary, looking bright and cheerful for a change, and waving a sheaf of papers in his hand.

"Guess what, guys?" he said as everybody turned his way. "I've got everybody's stats for the season right here.

You guys can check out how you're doing, and maybe do something to improve the areas where you're pathetic."

That last comment was meant as a joke, of course. A bunch of the kids cracked up as they reached for their personal stats sheets and started to look them over.

"That's great work, Gary!" Chase said, clapping him on the back. "Who gave you that idea?"

"I came up with it on my own, all by my little old self." Gary was standing right beside Derek when he said it, and Derek was about to say, "Hey, what about me?" when Gary gave him a quick wink, then turned away and continued giving out the stats sheets.

Chase must have noticed, because he turned to Derek and said, "What have you been saying to that boy?"

For the sake of team harmony, Derek decided to let Gary take the credit. "I just worked with him on his fielding, and Dad showed him how to hit. Maybe it affected his attitude. I don't know. I just hope it helps in the field."

"Good job!" Chase clapped him on the shoulder. "That's being a really good teammate."

Derek felt great hearing that. It was just how he wanted to see himself on this team that needed so much help. He knew his dad would be proud too, if he learned about all the work Derek had been doing with Gary and Dave.

That reminded Derek. . . . "Chase?"

"Yes?"

"Do you think you could get my dad to give Dave another

shot at pitching? I've been working with him, too, and he's gotten really good."

There. He'd managed to get up the courage to ask Chase at least, even though he couldn't bring himself to ask his dad directly.

"I'm going to leave those kinds of decisions to the head coach, Derek," Chase said. "I'm sure he'll give Dave another chance eventually. Hey, you might even find *yourself* back out on the mound."

Derek wanted to scream, "Noooo!" Pitching was the last thing he wanted to do on this team. But he kept silent.

As the team warmed up, going through infield practice before the game, Derek kept thinking there had to be a way to get his dad to give Dave another shot.

But how?

Derek knew from his stats sheet that he was leading the team in hitting with a .462 batting average. His slugging percentage was also high, at .631, showing that he'd hit a few doubles and triples, and even a couple of home runs.

The point was, the team counted on him as its best hitter. And from what he could see of the Giants' starting pitcher, Derek ought to be able to do some damage if the Indians could get hitters on base in front of him.

But Mason and Dean, while they made good contact, hit the ball right at two of the Giants' outfielders. So when Derek came to the plate, there were two outs and nobody on base.

Derek knew Dave was up next. Dave's average was only .325, but his slugging percentage was even higher than Derek's. Derek figured if he could get on, Dave might be able to drive him in. That would give the Indians the early lead—but even more important, it would give them hope that they could hang in there against the mighty Giants.

Derek let the first two pitches go by for strikes, but he watched them carefully, timing them so he would be ready for the next strike.

After trying to get Derek to swing at one in the dirt, the pitcher threw his fastest ball right over the heart of the plate.

Derek whacked it, and the ball took off, a screaming line drive that split the outfielders. Derek was on his horse at once, speeding around the base paths. Between second and third he saw that the throw back in had gotten away from the shortstop. Chase, who was acting as third base coach, waved his arm around frantically, signaling for Derek to keep on going.

Derek's heart was hammering in his chest, and he was gasping for breath, but he kept his speed up and slid into home a split second before the ball got there.

He'd done it! His fourth home run of the season, and a 1–0 Indians lead in the first!

He hadn't even needed Dave to drive him in. But Dave was up there to hit too, and he drove one to deep right that ricocheted off the glove of the right fielder.

Now it was Dave who came barreling around third. But one thing Dave hadn't practiced was sliding. He came in standing up and was tagged out by the catcher for the final out of the inning.

"Hey, that's okay," Mr. Jeter yelled, clapping encouragement. "Nice hitting anyway, Dave! Let's go, team. We've got a lead. Let's keep it!"

Easier said than done. Jonathan immediately had his hands full with the Giants' hitters. After he gave up a single and a walk, their next batter hit a shot over Vijay's head in left, scoring two runs.

Two walks and a single later, it was 4–1, Giants. Jonathan got lucky with a double play and a throw-out at the plate. But now the Indians were down again, by three big runs.

It was a steep hill to climb. But as their coaches reminded the Indians, it was still early. And soon the team showed they weren't going to go down easily.

It was Gary, hitting seventh today, who got them back on the scoreboard, cracking a long double to score Tito and Paul, who'd gotten on in front of him with a pair of walks.

That made the score 4–3, Giants, but Jonathan gave up two more runs in the bottom of the inning, putting the Indians back down by three.

Still, the team showed they weren't done yet, mounting another rally in their half of the third.

Derek was right in the middle of it, legging out an RBI triple, and then stealing home on the catcher's slow throw back to the mound. That bit of daring took everyone by surprise, causing the Giants' players to throw up their hands in frustration, and making the Indians' bench stand up and cheer.

Derek saw that even Gary was jumping up and down! *Maybe there's hope for him after all,* Derek thought as he high-fived teammates and got congrats from his dad and Chase. Hey, if Gary had become a believer, how could you count the Indians out?

From the beginning of the game the score had been seesawing, with the Indians putting runs up, and Jonathan giving them back. The Giants' hitters were making good on their fearsome reputation by pounding his pitches, inning after inning.

By the bottom of the fifth, it was tied, 7–7, but the Giants had the bases loaded, with two outs and their cleanup man at the plate.

Standing at shortstop, pounding his glove, Derek wished his dad would come out to the mound and give Dave the ball. But Mr. Jeter didn't know about all the progress Dave had made under Derek's coaching. As far as Derek's dad was concerned, Jonathan might have had his flaws, but he was still the best pitcher the team had.

Sweat was dripping down Jonathan's face. Derek knew how nervous he had to be, and shouted encouragement to him. Jonathan nodded back, showing he was listening. He reared back and threw his best heater. The batter made solid contact, sending the ball flying out to right field.

Gary was positioned perfectly, because Derek had taught him how to shift for lefties and play deep for power hitters.

Gary looked up, shielding his eyes from the sun with his mitt, just as Derek had shown him. At the last moment he ducked, but he kept his glove up and open—and somehow the ball found it!

Gary clamped his mitt shut with both hands, and the umpire signaled the out that ended the inning and kept the score tied!

Everyone cheered as Gary trotted back to the bench. Now it was his turn to get high-fived, and he sure seemed to be enjoying it. He nodded and strutted, and acted like he'd had that ball all the way.

Derek had to laugh. Was this the same kid who'd nearly brought the team to its knees with all his negativity the first three weeks of the season?

It sure didn't look like it. This was the first time Gary had been made to feel part of the team, and Derek knew how great that had to feel to Gary.

"Come on, Indians!" Chase shouted. "We've got these guys nervous! They haven't had a close game all year till now!"

"That's right," said Mr. Jeter. "If we take the lead now, they're going to start worrying!"

Derek hoisted his bat and headed to the plate to lead off the top of the sixth. Glancing over to the bench, he caught sight of Gary, who tipped his cap and nodded, pointing to him as if to say, *You're the man!*

Derek tipped his batting helmet in a return salute and settled into the batter's box. He scanned the field and saw that the outfielders were playing him to pull the ball. So he made up his mind to hit it to the opposite field if he could—in other words, to hit it where they *weren't*. Something else his dad had taught him over the years.

He fouled off three pitches in a row, took two that were out of the strike zone, then fouled off three more trying to go the other way.

If the Giants' coaches saw what he was trying to do, they didn't make their fielders adjust. So Derek kept to his plan, and on the next pitch he dinked one over the first baseman's head.

The ball landed just fair, and just far enough in the outfield for Derek to leg out a leadoff double!

With the go-ahead run at second, Dave's job was to knock him in. But Dave hit into bad luck. The second baseman grabbed his line drive with a last-second dive. Derek had to hustle back to the base to avoid making the second out.

Tito struck out, and Paul walked. That brought Gary up

to the plate with two on and two out. Derek knew this was the biggest at bat of the game so far. If the Indians didn't score now, the Giants could win the game in the bottom of the sixth against whomever Mr. Jeter put in to replace Jonathan, who by league rules had reached his pitching limit.

Gary waggled the bat over his shoulder, leaning back toward the catcher, with all his weight on his back foot, just like Mr. Jeter had taught him at the cages. He swung through the first pitch, which was way over his head.

"Easy, Gar!" Mr. Jeter yelled. "Make him throw you a strike!"

Gary nodded to show he'd heard, and got ready. Here came the pitch. . . .

Gary swung, and hit a grounder between the first and second basemen. Both tried to catch it, and it bounced off the first baseman's mitt. Meanwhile, the pitcher was late covering first base. Gary, slow runner that he was, beat out the throw to first—barely, huffing and puffing like a locomotive.

Meanwhile Derek, who had rounded third, saw that everyone's attention was on first base, and he just kept going.

"Home! Home!" the Giants' catcher yelled. The pitcher, who was holding the ball, saw what was happening and fired it in. Derek slid, and the tag came right on his helmet.

"Safe!" yelled the umpire.

"YEAH!" yelled the entire Indians bench.

The next batter struck out to end the rally, but now the Indians led, 8–7, and the Giants were down to their last licks.

Sure enough, they seemed tight and nervous, just as Chase and Mr. Jeter had predicted. Paul, the Indians' new pitcher, was finding it hard to get the ball over the plate, but that was just as well, since the hitters seemed anxious and overeager to swing.

Swinging at balls, not strikes, the first hitter dribbled a grounder back to the mound for an out. The second man up lined out to Derek, who made a spectacular leap to grab it before it went into the outfield.

Then the Giants' coach called his team together. Derek knew he had to be telling his hitters to make Paul throw strikes, that a walk right now was as good as a hit.

The next two men walked, and Mr. Jeter walked out to the mound and took the ball from Paul, who looked dejected. "Derek!" he called.

Derek blinked in shock. *No!* he thought. *Not me! Not now!*

"Dad," he said as he reached the mound. He was about to say something about giving Dave a try, but his dad never gave him the chance.

"Just get us one out, Son," he said, handing Derek the ball. "I *know* you can do it."

Derek nodded, took a deep breath, and accepted the fact that he had no choice but to get this done. He reared back and threw the ball as hard as he could. But his first three pitches missed badly, and he wound up walking the first man he faced.

Now the bases were loaded. He couldn't afford to walk this next guy, or the Indians' lead would be gone, and with it their best chance of winning the game.

So Derek took a little speed off his fastball, concentrating instead on getting it over and hoping that his fielders would make a play behind him if the batter made good contact.

On a 1–1 count the hitter smacked a high fly deep to right. Gary got a good jump on it, took the perfect route to the ball, and, miracle of miracles, reached out and grabbed it one-handed to end the game!

In the celebration that followed, there were no pranks from Gary, no snide negative comments, no put-upon sighs or rolling eyes—only high fives, cheers, and hugs from his teammates.

Their coaches were ecstatic too. "Gary, you get the game ball!" said Mr. Jeter, and everyone cheered again.

"I'm going to have to revise all those crummy stats," Gary cracked, and everyone laughed.

Derek felt deeply happy. Not only had his team finally *won* a game, but he'd contributed in a number of areas. Gary might have been awarded the game ball, but Derek knew he'd had a whole lot to do with Gary's improved fielding.

Not to mention that, at 1–3, the Indians had a pulse. They'd beaten the mighty, previously unbeaten Giants! Now the Indians could at least hope this was the beginning of better times for the team, with more wins to come in the future.

All that, thought Derek, *plus* he was going to get a great grade on his math project!

Chapter Thirteen
THE ROAD BACK

"*A-plus!* Ha!"

Gary waved his and Derek's project paper high in the air for everyone to see. Derek was almost embarrassed by this public display of their success. After all, it was meant as much to make the other kids feel *bad* as to make Gary and Derek feel *good*.

"What did *you* get, Hennum?" Gary asked Dave, who was examining his and Teresa's paper. "B-minus? Aww, that's too bad."

"Buzz off, Parnell," said Dave, clearly irritated.

"Bzzzzz. . . . I'm buzzing. But it's *you* who got the 'bee.'"

"Hey, knock it off, Gar," said Derek, sensitive to his best friend's feelings, and tired of Gary's constant needling.

"Just be happy with our grade, and quit rubbing it in. Nobody likes that."

"That's the point," said Gary with a satisfied smile on his face. "What good is winning if you can't enjoy your triumph at other people's expense?"

"It's the *expense* part that stinks, actually," said Derek, who could see that Dave was sulking. "You should apologize."

"Dream on, Jeter. You know, I don't understand why you always hang out with those jocks you call your friends. You may not be as dumb as you look—or as dumb as your friends *are*—but they're just dragging you down."

"They're *not* dumb! And oh, by the way, I hope you notice that you and I make pretty good teammates. We don't have to compete against each other, you know. It's not like it's a rule or anything."

"Don't get carried away," said Gary, making a sour face. "We might have aced this project together, but you're still the competition in my book. And you should be flattered. At least you have enough intelligence to give me a run for my money once in a while."

Derek laughed. He wasn't about to let Gary annoy him, not when the two of them had just gotten the best mark in the whole class, and not when Gary had finally started to act like a team member on the Indians.

Besides, what did it matter if he and Gary never became friends? Gary had the competitive spirit, that was for sure—

same as Derek—and either way, compete or cooperate, they seemed to make each other perform better.

Still, for the sake of the Indians, Derek hoped Gary would continue to act like a decent teammate, at least for the rest of the season. The Indians, he knew, would keep winning only if every member of the team pulled his weight, and pulled *together*.

Today the Indians were scheduled to play the Nationals. The boys all seemed excited to be there, and Derek knew it was because they'd finally tasted victory, and beaten the best team in the league too. In short, they had begun to believe in themselves.

Derek's dad was talking to the other team's coach before the game, and Derek noticed that he'd left his scorebook on the bench.

Knowing his dad wouldn't like it if he saw Derek looking, but unable to resist taking a peek, Derek examined today's lineup—and was shocked to see that he was slated to be the team's starting pitcher!

He quickly stepped back from the bench to avoid being seen. But he couldn't hide his shock.

Derek had to make him consider Dave, even if his dad got mad at him for pleading on Dave's behalf. Taking a deep breath, Derek started over there, determined to speak up before it was too late for the team.

But then he had a flash—remembering a phrase he'd

heard once from his teacher, who'd been commenting on some assignment or other where they were supposed to explain things in front of the class.

"Show, don't tell," Ms. Fein had said. Derek had forgotten all about it till now, but suddenly it had come back into his head.

And that gave him a great idea. . . .

"Dave!" he said, turning to his friend, who'd been penciled in at third base as usual, and who already had his glove on, ready to start taking infield practice. "Come here!"

"What's up?"

"Pitch to me!"

"Huh? *Now?* It's almost game time."

"Now!"

"What for?"

"Don't ask questions. Just . . . just trust me, okay?"

Dave shrugged. "Okay."

"Get out to the mound," Derek ordered.

"Uh, why don't we just go into the outfield or someplace? I don't want to be in the way of the pitcher getting his warm-ups."

"The pitcher is me," Derek said. "And you won't be getting in my way. Just trust me, okay? Get on out there and throw me everything you've got."

Shaking his head in confusion, Dave reluctantly went out to the mound. Derek grabbed the team's catcher's mitt before Miles got to it, and crouched down behind the plate, giving Dave a target.

Dave started throwing his heater—once, twice, three times—then threw a changeup, before hurling another fastball, right on the corner of the plate.

"Hey!" It was Miles in his catcher's gear, coming up to Derek. "I need my mitt, Derek. I've gotta warm you up. Your dad just said you're pitching today."

"Maybe I am, maybe I'm not," said Derek.

"Come on, give me the mitt," said Miles impatiently.

"Just a couple more minutes. Come on, Dave. Right here." Derek pounded the catcher's mitt and stuck it out, making a perfect target for Dave to aim at.

"What's going on over here?" said Mr. Jeter, suddenly aware that Derek was hogging home plate. "Derek, I've got you pitching today, not catching."

Derek didn't answer. "Throw me the changeup," he called to Dave.

Dave threw it, and Derek's dad saw that the pitch was as tricky as it was supposed to be. "Huh," he said thoughtfully. "Do that again, Dave."

Dave threw another one. "Nice," said Mr. Jeter. "Very nice. You've been working on that one, haven't you?"

"Yessir," Dave said.

"How's your fastball?"

Dave threw one to show him. It was on the corner and at the knees.

"Give me one up high," said Mr. Jeter. Dave did as he was told.

"Wow. I've got to say, you've really improved, Dave. Good going."

After taking his pencil from behind his ear, where he'd been stowing it, he scratched something into his scorebook. "You know what? I think we're going to slot *you* in as starting pitcher today. Let's see how you do."

"Yesss!" said Dave and Derek together.

"What about me, Dad? I mean, Coach?" asked Derek.

"I'll shift Jonathan over to third. You can take over at short."

"Yesss!" Derek said again. "Thanks, Coach!"

Chase came over to see what was going on. Mr. Jeter cocked his head. "I don't suppose it was you who worked with Dave on his pitching?" he asked.

"Not me," said Chase, who had clearly been watching the whole thing. He gave Derek a quick wink.

"Not me either," said Mr. Jeter. He looked at Derek and Dave, who looked at each other and shrugged, pretending not to know anything. But Derek knew they weren't fooling anybody.

"Here," said Derek, giving the catcher's mitt to Miles as the coaches walked back to the bench. "You can take over from here. Make sure you have him throw change-ups whenever the hitter's expecting a fastball."

"Got it," said Miles. "Hey, Derek?"

"Yeah?"

"It was *you*, right?"

Derek gave him a wink. "I don't know what you're talking about," he said, and they both shared a laugh. "Let's go get 'em today."

"Right on," said Miles, crouching down and pounding his mitt as he prepared to finish warming Dave up for the game.

Derek got his own mitt and trotted out to short, feeling mighty pleased with himself.

Now if only Dave can take advantage of the opportunity . . .

All Derek could do was watch and stay ready in case the ball was hit to him. Dave was doing the rest. He made the first two Nationals hitters look helpless, getting two quick strikes with his fastball, then finishing both off with his changeup.

Cheers went up from the fielders behind him with each strikeout, and Dave seemed to gain confidence with each swing and miss.

The third batter hit a fastball, looping it over Derek's head. Derek ran back on the ball, then leapt at the last minute and snagged it—and held on as he landed hard on the grass.

"Woo-hoo!" Vijay shouted out in left field. "Derek Jeter! I think you are ready for the New York Yankees right now!"

Derek grinned as he got up, threw the ball in, and trot-ted back to the bench, shaking his head. "Come on, Vij. Cut it out," he said.

Vijay knew it was Derek's dream to start at shortstop for the Yankees, and when Vijay believed in something, he believed it with his whole heart.

That was one of the things Derek liked best about him. But sometimes he wished Vijay wouldn't say some of the things he did. It just embarrassed Derek to have people talk about the dreams he was striving for.

Mason led off for the Indians in the bottom of the first, and promptly got hit by a pitch. "Ow!" he said, rubbing his butt where the ball had plunked him. "That hurt!"

"You okay, Mason?" Chase called out.

"I guess," said Mason, who had been limping toward first but suddenly seemed able to walk normally.

Dean was up next. He grounded out to first, but Mason made it to second base in spite of his sore rear end. Now it was Derek's turn to hit.

The Nationals' pitcher was a real fireballer, which explained Mason's sore butt. But Derek had never been afraid of the ball, or even of being hit by a pitch. So when the ball came straight at him, he calmly ducked, then got right back into the batter's box, ready to give as good as he got.

The next pitch came in over the outside corner, and Derek was ready. He went the other way with it, slapping it right over the first baseman's head.

Derek steamed around first and headed for second. When the throw came in to the plate, too late to nail Mason, Derek kept on going and slid safely into third before the throw got there!

Dave was up next, and he didn't disappoint. On the very first pitch, he clubbed one to deep center field. The Nationals' outfielder sped back and grabbed it with a fine catch, but Derek tagged up and came in easily to score the Indians' second run.

Dave's shot was the only hard-hit ball the Indians managed during the first four innings. But the score stayed 2–0 because Dave, who had settled into a great rhythm, was keeping the Nationals' hitters off balance with his changes of speed.

He wasn't walking anybody either. He would throw balls off the plate, both inside and out, both high and low. But because his pitches were close to being strikes, the hitters were fooled and went after them, and ended up missing or making weak contact.

"Amazing!" Mr. Jeter crowed when Dave came back to the bench after the top of the fifth. "How are you holding up, Dave?"

"I'm fine," Dave said, nodding and smiling. But Derek noticed—and he was sure his dad did too—that Dave was rubbing his right biceps when he thought no one was looking.

Well, thought Derek, it was no wonder that Dave was

getting tired and his arm was starting to feel sore. He wasn't used to throwing this many pitches—not even close. Derek wondered if Dave's fatigue would start to show late in the game, and what would happen if it did.

The Indians put two men on in the fifth—one on a walk, the other on a hit batsman. The Nationals' pitcher was still throwing fire, but his control was starting to go out the window as he too began to tire.

With two out Derek came to the plate, knowing that if he could somehow drive the runners in, the Indians would have a commanding lead going into the sixth and last inning.

He swung at the first pitch and hit a screaming line drive, but the pitcher reached out his mitt and snagged it!

Derek groaned and grabbed his batting helmet with both hands. The pitcher groaned too, shaking his glove hand out and wincing in pain.

The inning was over, and the Indians were going to have to protect their slim two-run lead for three more outs.

Dave took the mound and started throwing his warm-up pitches. But it was easy to see he'd lost his command. Every pitch was wild; not one came near the plate.

When he walked the first hitter on four pitches, Mr. Jeter came out to the mound and took the ball from him. "Outstanding work, Dave," Derek heard him say. "I think we've found ourselves a new ace, but enough's enough for one day."

He turned toward Derek, and Derek was afraid his dad was about to ask him to take over, but Mr. Jeter called for Jonathan instead, and sent Dave to the bench, putting Paul at third base.

Now the tying run was at the plate, with nobody out, and Derek was starting to get nervous. The Nationals were 4–1 on the season so far, with their only loss coming to the Giants. With a pitcher like they had, it was no wonder they had such a good record, Derek thought. Dave had held his own, but he'd run out of gas one inning too early.

In games to come Dave would be more used to pitching. He'd be stronger and better able to continue, but that was no help today. And today's game meant *everything*. If they lost after leading the whole game, all their momentum and good feelings about themselves would be gone!

Jonathan's fastball was not as hard or accurate as Dave's, and he had no changeup to keep the hitters off balance. The second batter shot a hard grounder between the second and first basemen for a single, sending the runner all the way to third.

The next hitter popped out to Paul, and the ball was too shallow for the runner at third to score. Derek breathed a sigh of relief. But the Indians were hanging on by their fingernails, and it was going to take some luck to win this game.

The cleanup man came up to bat, with murder in his eyes. He swung so hard at the first pitch that he nearly came out of his shoes, but the rocket he hit fell just foul of the right field line for a long, loud strike one.

"Get him, Johnnie!" came a voice from right field. *Gary.* Derek had to smile. Gary's fierce competitiveness and drive to win was overcoming his usual obnoxiousness. And *that* inspired Vijay, Dave, and the others to join in, loudly yelling for Jonathan to strike the big guy out.

Jonathan must have heard them, because he reared back and threw his fastest pitch of the season. The hitter missed, and suddenly the count was 0–2.

"One more!" Gary yelled from the outfield. "Come on, get him!"

Again the team roared encouragement in response.

Jonathan geared up and fired another heater. But by now the hitter had timed his swing enough to catch up with the pitch.

He hit a long shot to left, but Vijay had been playing him deep and was able to catch up with the ball and make a running grab.

"Yeah!" Derek yelled, thrusting his arms into the air, even as the runner at third tagged up and scored the Nationals' first run, cutting the Indians' lead in half.

It was a play Vijay could never have made in years past. But over the last few weeks Mr. Jeter and Chase had taught him to play the outfield with his mind as well as his body. By putting himself into a better position, and taking better routes to the ball, he'd become a decent outfielder.

Derek felt really proud of him. Nobody worked harder on his game, or cared more, than Vijay.

Now there were two outs and a man on first. Jonathan walked the next batter, and the Nationals were just a single away from tying the game—or a double away from taking the lead!

Jonathan quickly went 2-and-0 on the hitter. "Just get it over, Johnnie," Derek called to the mound. "Let him make contact. We've got your back!"

Jonathan nodded and stared in at the catcher, determined to throw a strike. The hitter dug into the batter's box, knowing a fastball was coming right down the middle.

The batter hit it as hard as a grounder can be hit, so hard that it made Jonathan duck out of the way instead of trying to field it.

Derek reacted instinctively, moving to his left and speeding behind second base. He reached out and snared the ball, but his momentum was carrying him into right field. He knew he had no chance to catch the runner at first, and if he tried, he might throw the ball away and let the tying run score!

But in that split second his instincts took over, and he flipped the ball behind his back to second base, where Mason was standing, glove outstretched, foot on the bag. The ball sank into his mitt a moment before the runner's foot hit.

"OUT!" cried the ump.

The game was over! They'd done it! And Derek had made the defensive play of the season to nail down the victory, just when the win had been about to slip out of their grasp!

As the team celebrated their second straight win, Derek and Dave were right in the middle of the pile.

"Awesome!" cried Derek, high-fiving his best friend.

"Thanks, Chief!" Dave replied.

"This game ball belongs to you, Mr. MVP."

"How 'bout we share it?" Derek suggested.

"Sounds good," said Dave, and the two friends high-fived again.

"You know what?" Derek said. "I've got a feeling this is the beginning of a beautiful winning streak."

Chapter Fourteen
HOME STRETCH

May turned to June, and the weather began to feel like summer. All the students at Saint Augustine's school were studying hard for their finals, especially Derek. Mr. Jeter had finished his year of teaching at Western Michigan University and was studying for his doctoral degree.

Sharlee's T-ball team was undefeated and, with one game left, was firmly in first place, just as she had predicted so confidently back in early May. And the Indians kept on winning.

After a long hot streak, they were now 7–4, with just one big game left to play. Big because if they won it, they'd be in the playoffs!

Under a new system adopted by the league for this year,

the top six teams would make the playoffs. If the Indians beat the Dodgers, they would finish sixth. If they lost . . .

Well, that was not going to happen! Derek was confident about that. The Indians were playing like a well-oiled machine, and had been for the past four weeks. They were 5–0 in that time span.

Thanks to Gary's stat-keeping—which he'd continued, even after his and Derek's project had been handed in—everyone on the team could see where he stood and where he needed improvement.

Chase and Mr. Jeter had come into their own as coaches, working with each individual team member on his skills and keeping the team focused and in high spirits.

It was a situation Derek could not even have dreamed of being in early in the season, when they'd been 0–3 and struggling to find unity and focus. The Indians—as a team, as individual players, as coaches—had been through some serious growing pains. But they'd grown together to get past their troubles and find success.

Still, all of that could go right down the drain if they lost their next game, and everyone on the team knew it. Derek could feel the tightness in his jaw and the uneasiness in his mood. There was unfinished business, and until it was finished, no one on the Indians could relax.

That afternoon Derek sat in the stands and watched Sharlee lead her team to an undefeated season and a T-ball championship. As he sat there, cheering her on along with his parents, Derek thought back to the beginning of both their seasons, when she had kept on bragging about her team and her accomplishments, and he had had to bite down on his tongue rather than say something he'd regret later.

Because that was what had been on his mind, to say, "Stop bragging! Can't you see it only makes me feel worse about my own crummy team?"

Well, he hadn't said it, and now he was glad—for Sharlee and for himself. He'd made sure to be there for her last three games, even though it had cost him time on the Hill with his friends.

Some things were just more important than others, he reflected now, and he was glad he'd shown up for his sister, because after all, family came first.

After the game Sharlee celebrated with her teammates, then made a beeline for Derek and leapt into his arms and hugged him even before giving her parents hugs.

Derek felt like a million dollars for being a good big brother, even though he knew he could have been a better one early in the season. He promised himself that next year, no matter what was going on with his own team, he'd be there for Sharlee from the very beginning of her season.

"Mommy, Daddy, can Ciara come over for another overnight?" Sharlee begged.

"Sure, honey—if it's all right with her parents," said Mrs. Jeter. "Right, Jeter?"

"Right, Dot," agreed Mr. Jeter.

"Hey, Mom? Dad?" Derek broke in. "Dave and I have been talking about an overnight for a while. Do you think—"

"Don't you have a lot of studying to do this next week?" asked his mom.

"We could study together," Derek suggested.

"Jeter?" his mom asked his dad.

Mr. Jeter looked thoughtful. "I'll speak to Chase about it," he said, which was good enough for Derek.

He was sure Chase would say yes. He was a big fan of the Jeter family, and of Derek in particular. Why would he say no?

"Now let's get home," said Mr. Jeter. "Derek and I both have studying to do. Come on, Sharlee."

"Wait! I have to go get my trophy!" she cried, and ran back to huddle with her teammates, who were gathering around their coach in anticipation. Soon she ran back to join them, with a trophy in each hand. "Look!" she said, her eyes wide with ecstasy. "I'm the most valuable player!"

"Wow! Good for you, Sharlee!" Derek said, hugging her again.

"Here, Mommy. Hold these," she said, handing the trophies over. "Can I go with the team to Jahn's for ice cream? Pleeease?"

All the Jeters laughed. When Sharlee turned on the charm, she was pretty irresistible.

"Sure. Why not?" said Mr. Jeter. "In fact, we'll all go. *Most valuable player?* That deserves a celebration!"

The next day at school Derek wanted to ask Dave about an overnight, but Dave found him first, and was he ever excited.

"Guess what?" he said. "My parents are coming home!"

"Wow! Both of them?"

"Yeah, and for a while!"

"Great. When?"

"I think they're going to be here tonight, but it might be tomorrow. I'm a little confused, because where *they* are, it's *already* tomorrow. Something about the international date line."

"Huh?"

"I know. I don't understand it either. But Chase says they might make it to the game tomorrow."

"Fantastic!"

"I know. I hope they do. I want them to see me pitch!"

Dave's confidence was understandable. Ever since Mr. Jeter had put him back in as starting pitcher, the changeup Derek had taught him had only gotten better, making Dave's fastball almost unhittable. As much as anything else, it was the reason the Indians had gone on a tear, winning seven of their last eight games.

If Dave was feeling confident about pitching tomorrow in front of his parents, he had every reason to be. It was easy to envision the Indians beating the mighty Dodgers, who had the second-best record in the whole league and were going to the playoffs for sure, even if they lost.

"How long are they going to be here for?"

Dave's eyes widened with excitement. "That's the best part. My mom said she'll be home for at least a couple of months, and my dad for even longer than that."

"Wow, Dave, that's so great. I'm really happy for you."

He was, too. It had always been hard for Derek to imagine how Dave dealt with his parents being away most of the time on business, and having someone else be in charge of him, no matter how great a guy Chase was.

"Yeah, me too. I can't wait for them to meet you and your folks."

"Give me five on that," said Derek, raising his hand for a slap. "Hey, I was meaning to ask you—my folks said it's okay if we have an overnight next week, as long as it's okay with Chase."

"Great!" Dave said. "Of course, now it'll be up to my *folks*, but I'm sure that won't be a problem. Chase has already told them about you guys, and I know they're psyched to meet you."

Derek felt relieved, although he couldn't have said why. Chase was someone he knew and liked a lot, and who already liked him back. He sure hoped Dave's parents would feel the same way, but still, Derek knew it was up to him to make a good first impression. He would have to put his best foot forward tomorrow, both in the game and on the sidelines when he met Mr. and Mrs. Hennum.

"Don't worry. It's a done deal. I'm sure of it," Dave said. "Just let's get a win tomorrow, so my folks can root for us all the way through the playoffs!"

Chapter Fifteen

DO OR DIE

"Anybody seen Dave?" Mr. Jeter looked around at the team, assembled in front of him. "Or Coach Bradway?"

Everyone looked at one another. No one had seen either of them. Mr. Jeter checked his watch. "Hmmm. They're usually here by now. I wonder what—"

Just then the familiar Mercedes sedan rolled slowly down the drive and pulled up by the side of the field. Chase emerged and opened the rear door. A lady got out, thanked Chase, and, shading her eyes from the sun, looked around at the scene.

Meanwhile Chase ran around to the other side of the car. He opened that door too, and a handsome, tall man emerged—followed by Dave, who'd been sitting in the front seat. The man put his arm around Dave's shoulders and said something to him, and Dave beamed.

"Those must be Dave's parents!" Derek said. And here they came. Dave was practically pulling his mom's hand, so excited was he to introduce her and his dad to the team.

"Hi, everybody!" he called as they approached. "Sorry we're late."

"My fault, I'm afraid," Chase said. "I was a little late getting to the airport. Coach, everybody—I'd like to introduce Mr. and Mrs. Hennum, Dave's parents."

"How do you do?" said Mrs. Hennum, with a smile that seemed halfhearted to Derek. He figured it must have been because she'd just gotten off an airplane after a long flight and had come straight here instead of to her home.

"Nice to meet you all," said Mr. Hennum, with a nod to the team members.

"Hi," some of the Indians replied.

"And this," said Chase, "is Charles Jeter, Dave's coach. And an excellent one, in my opinion."

"A pleasure," said Dave's mom, offering her hand, but in a way that looked like she wanted it kissed instead of shaken.

Derek's dad shook it anyway. "Pleasure's mine," he said with a warm smile. "Dave's a fine young man. You must be very proud."

"We are," said Mr. Hennum, putting an arm around Dave and nodding to Mr. Jeter. "Thank you. I hope he's behaved himself."

"Oh, yes, definitely."

"And this," said Chase, "is Charles's son, Derek—Dave's best friend, as I told you."

"Oh. Yes. How do you do?" said Mrs. Hennum, looking Derek up and down in a way that made him feel distinctly uncomfortable.

"Nice to meet you," said Derek, giving her his best smile.

"Indeed," she replied, still looking taken aback.

"Hello there, young man." Mr. Hennum nodded to Derek and gave what could have passed for a smile but certainly wasn't much of one.

"Hi, Mr. Hennum." Derek wasn't sure if he should offer his hand. He decided, just on instinct, not to.

"Derek taught me practically everything I know about baseball!" Dave said excitedly. "And Mr. Jeter too, of course."

"Is that so?" said Mrs. Hennum, still looking doubtful. "Well, we're looking forward to seeing you play, David." Turning to Chase, she asked, "Where shall we sit?"

"Most folks sit over there," Chase said, indicating the hard metal bleachers along the third-base line. Then, seeing the look of disgust that came over her face, he added, "But I brought you a couple of folding chairs, if you'd prefer . . ."

"Yes, please," she said, giving him a smile that was clearly just for show. "And put them over there," she added, pointing to the first-base line.

Hmmm. Derek could see that the Hennums felt

uncomfortable mixing with the team members and their families. He remembered back to when Dave had first moved to Kalamazoo, and how he, too, had kept himself aloof from everyone, until Derek had finally broken through his standoffishness. Seeing Dave's parents, Derek could see where Dave got that quality.

He sure hoped they would warm up to him and his family, the way Dave had.

Dave, for his part, seemed not to notice the chill in the air at all. He was practically jumping up and down, so eager was he to get out on the mound and start the game.

Derek hoped that the seventy-five pitches Dave was limited to would be enough for the whole game, but he had his doubts. The Dodgers were a high-scoring team and had worn pitchers out all season.

Taking grounders at short to warm up, Derek kept glancing over at Dave's parents, who were seated in their folding chairs along the first-base side, a good distance from all the other family members and friends who had come to cheer both teams on.

Even so, they leaned in toward each other when they spoke, as if they didn't want people to overhear them, as if anyone *could* from that far away.

Derek couldn't help wondering what they were saying. They sure weren't in the same excited mood as everybody else. Maybe they were just tired from their flights, he guessed. Or maybe they didn't like any sports except golf.

The game began, and Dave started right in with two of his best fastballs. The Dodgers' leadoff man swung at and missed both. Then Dave followed up with a nasty changeup, and the hitter, way out in front, whiffed.

"Woo-hoo!" Derek yelled. "Great job, Dave!"

Glancing over at Dave's folks again, he saw them both clapping proudly but politely, as if they were watching a golf tournament or something. Obviously they weren't baseball fans, but that was no surprise. When he'd first gotten to town, Dave had never played baseball in his life, only golf.

The next pitch came so fast that Derek was startled when the ball was hit right at him. He fumbled the sharp grounder, a ball he normally would have scooped up with no problem, and by the time he recovered it, there was no chance to nail the runner at first.

"Rats!" he muttered under his breath, mad at himself for letting his attention wander. Now he'd made an error—only his second of the season, but it couldn't have come at a worse moment. The Indians needed this game! How could he have let them down like that?

Now, with a man on first, things got more tense. The runner took off for second on Dave's 1–0 pitch, and beat the throw to Derek, for a stolen base. When the hitter flied out to right, the runner tagged up and went to third.

With two out, the cleanup man swung at Dave's first pitch and dinked a pop fly behind Derek. He raced back to catch it, but it was just far enough away to elude his grasp. The runner scored, and the Dodgers had a 1–0 lead on an unearned run, thanks to Derek's error.

He moped back to the bench after Dave struck out the next hitter. "Come on, come on, keep your chin up," said his dad, clapping him on the shoulder. "It's still early. We'll get 'em back."

Derek nodded and forced himself to focus on his upcoming at bat.

His dad was right. Baseball was a game of redemption. You could be struggling one moment, and a hero the next. It was only the first inning, after all. There was a lot of baseball left to play.

Mason led off with a walk, and right away Derek felt better. Dean singled to center, and Derek came up with men on first and third, and nobody out. "Go get them, Derek!" Vijay yelled. "Hit a home run!"

"Cream it, Derek!" Dave shouted, clapping, and the rest of the team started whooping it up too. Derek could feel their support and excitement as he stepped to the plate and tapped it with the end of his bat.

He let one pitch go by for a strike, just to get a feel for the speed of the pitch. Looking out at the field, he saw that the Dodgers, like most teams in the league, were playing him to pull the ball to the left side of the field. So he decided to cross them up by trying to hit it the other way.

The pitch came in, crowding him inside. Keeping his hands close to his body, Derek brought them through, then forced the bat through the hitting zone. He caught the ball square, and it sizzled through the hole between the second and first basemen, into the outfield, tying the game!

Reaching first, Derek clapped his hands together in triumph. "There!" he told himself. "At least I got us that run back. Let's go, Dave!"

Dave nodded at him and waggled his bat, ready to rumble. He hit a long fly ball to left that was caught, but Dean at third tagged up and scored to give the Indians the lead, 2–1.

Gary was the next man up. Mr. Jeter had moved him up to fifth in the order because he was hitting the ball so well lately. Sure enough, Gary smacked a base hit down the left-field line, scoring Derek for the team's third run!

"Attaway, Gary!" Derek screamed, pointing at his teammate and clapping for him. Gary tipped his cap in response, nodding as if he'd expected nothing less from himself.

On the next pitch Gary shocked everyone, most of all his teammates, by stealing second base, something he could never have done earlier in the season. He'd definitely gotten himself into better shape playing ball, just as his mom had intended when she'd forced him to participate in Little League.

Now it was Gary's turn to point at Derek. "Oh yeah!" he said, nodding cockily. "Now who's a speed demon?"

Derek laughed and clapped his hands as he shook his head in wonder. Was this the same Gary he'd always known and been annoyed by?

"Sheesh!" he said to Vijay, who was laughing and clapping too. "Can you believe him?"

"No way!" Vijay replied. "It's a real miracle!"

Tito struck out, but Paul bounced one over the pitcher's head and beat out the throw to first. Gary, who had reached third, just kept going and made it home before the startled first baseman realized what was happening.

By the end of the first inning, it was 4–1, Indians, and Derek and his teammates were determined to make that lead stand.

The score remained the same through the end of the fourth inning. Both teams put men on base, but the pitchers held firm, and the fielders made some great plays behind them.

In the top of the fifth, Dave struck out the first batter. But now he'd reached his pitch limit. Mr. Jeter walked out to the mound and took the ball from him, signaling to third base for Jonathan to come pitch the rest of the game.

Dave went to third, and Derek high-fived him. "Great going," he said. "Your folks'll be really proud of you."

"Thanks," said Dave, glancing over at them and waving. They waved back, but they didn't seem to know what was really going on in the game, or even whether their son had done well or not. Derek wondered if they knew the rules of baseball at all.

It quickly became obvious that Jonathan didn't have his best stuff today. He walked the first two guys he faced, and then gave up a double and a homer. Before he'd even gotten an out, the Indians were suddenly trailing, 5–4!

"Don't worry," Derek called out to him. "Just throw it over, and we'll take care of the rest!"

But Jonathan issued two more walks. The Dodgers' cleanup hitter came to the plate, swinging his bat like he wanted to smash something with it.

Derek exchanged worried glances with Dave over at third. Jonathan's first pitch was creamed, but luckily, it fell just foul, with Vijay desperately scrambling for it.

The next pitch was in the dirt, but the hitter laid off it. Two balls later, with the count 3–1, Jonathan threw one over the heart of the plate. The batter swung for all he was worth—and hit a screaming bouncer to Derek's right.

Derek lunged to grab it on one hop. Bouncing back up, he flung the ball to Dave, who stepped on third, then fired his best fastball to first base, just nipping the runner for the double play to end the inning!

They'd staved off total disaster, and now ran back to the bench to cheers from their teammates and coaches. But Derek knew the battle was far from won.

The Indians had only six outs to get a run back and tie the game. Time was running out on their season, and it was now or never if they wanted to make the playoffs.

The Indians' first two hitters both grounded out, and things were looking bleak.

Derek came to the plate, telling himself to be patient and wait for his pitch, and not try to do too much with it.

The team needed a base runner more than anything else, and Derek, while he had some power, was not really a home run hitter.

With the count 2–2, he fouled off three straight pitches, then sent a line drive over the second baseman's head for a single. Rounding the bag, he clapped his hands together so hard that it stung. "Yesss!" he cried.

Dave was next. He took the first two pitches. The second one was high and got away from the catcher. Derek wasted no time cruising into second on the wild pitch.

Dave made contact on the next pitch and hit a fly ball to shallow center. The shortstop, second baseman, and center fielder all yelled "I got it!" But none of them did. It dropped in for a single, and Derek, who had had to hold at second in case the ball had been caught, slid into third after the ball fell to the ground.

First and third, two men out, and Gary came to the plate. *Funny,* thought Derek. For the first half of the season, he would have dreaded seeing Gary come to bat in a situation like this.

But now everything was different. Gary was fitter than he'd ever been, and he'd been schooled in hitting by the best coach Derek had ever known.

All that hard work had to pay off. It just had to!

Derek clapped his hands and leaned toward home, one foot on the bag. "Let's go, Gar!" he shouted.

Gary gave him a nod and waggled the bat over his shoulder. In came the pitch. . . .

CRACK!

The ball sailed into the outfield, and the center fielder took off after it, but he had no chance. Derek and Dave both scored, and Gary wound up on third base, huffing and puffing but clapping his hands in triumph. "Woo-hoo!" he yelled back at his teammates, who were yelling the same thing at him.

The next man struck out, but now the Indians had a one-run lead. All they had to do was keep it for three more outs, and they were on their way to the playoffs!

"Derek!" called his dad. "Take the ball. You're pitching. Jonathan, take over at short."

Derek's heart sank, but only for a moment. He remembered his dad's telling him to be the best teammate he could be, no matter what job the coach gave him. His job now was to get three outs without giving up a run. And he was going to give it everything he had.

The Dodgers were good hitters, especially against the fastball. Derek started them out with slow changeups, just like the ones he'd taught Dave to throw. Mixing in the occasional fastball off the plate, he managed to strike out the first hitter and get the next to hit a grounder right back to him for the second out.

One more man, and it's over, he told himself.

Derek got strike one on a changeup, then tried to sneak a fastball by the hitter. . . .

Big mistake.

The hitter whacked it high and far, and Gary set off running, though he was still catching his breath from the triple he'd hit.

The ball fell in, but Gary was on it quickly and fired it back to Jonathan, the cutoff man. Jonathan relayed it in, throwing a pea right to the catcher just as the runner came barreling in!

The runner didn't think to slide, since he must have figured he'd be safe by a mile. His foot hit the plate an instant after Miles tagged him.

"Out!" the umpire yelled.

And it was *over*!

Derek tossed his glove high into the air as the whole team raced to the mound to celebrate their incredible comeback victory.

Dave hugged Derek, and the two boys jumped up and down. They were soon joined by Vijay, who was so happy he looked as though he would take off and fly.

Dave went over and hugged Chase, then ran to his parents to accept their congratulations.

Derek gave Chase a high five and thanked him for all of his help. Then he found his dad, who was beaming as he watched his team enjoying the fruits of all their hard work during the season.

"Dad!" Derek said. "Thank you soooo much! I knew if you coached my team, we'd win!"

"Did you?" his dad asked with a sly smile. "I have to

say, I had doubts myself. But you boys definitely made me proud. And you know what? It's not over yet!"

"You can say that again!" Derek crowed. "Hey, Coach—I mean, Dad?"

"Yes, Son?"

"I love you."

Mr. Jeter looked for a second like he was fighting back a tear or two. But he quickly recovered his composure. "Love you, too, Son. And I'm proud of you—for everything. On and off the field. Playing, and being a great teammate . . . the whole works. You keep it up, and there's no dream in the world you can't achieve."

Derek practically floated home, and stayed on a cloud the rest of that day. The whole season, so full of growing pains, kept flashing through his mind in a blur. But out of that whirlwind one thought kept coming back, loud and clear. *We're going to the playoffs, and we're going to win the championship!*

For now it was just a thought. But Derek was sure in his heart that *this* dream, at least, was going to come true.

INDIANS OPENING DAY ROSTER

Mason Adams—2B

Dean O'Leary—CF

Derek Jeter—C

Dave Hennum—P

Tito Ortega—1B

Paul Edwards—3B

Jonathan Hogue—SS

Vijay Patel—LF

Gary Parnell—RF

Reserves: Miles Kaufman, Eddie Falk,
Jonah Winters
Coaches: Charles Jeter and Chase Bradway

JETER'S LEADERS

is a leadership development program created to empower, recognize, and enhance the skills of high school students who:

- **PROMOTE HEALTHY LIFESTYLES AND ARE FREE OF ALCOHOL AND SUBSTANCE ABUSE**

- **ACHIEVE ACADEMICALLY**

- **ARE COMMITTED TO IMPROVING THEIR COMMUNITY THROUGH SOCIAL CHANGE ACTIVITIES**

- **SERVE AS ROLE MODELS TO YOUNGER STUDENTS AND DELIVER POSITIVE MESSAGES TO THEIR PEERS**

Photo credit: Eileen Barroso/Turn 2 Foundation, Inc.

"Your role models should teach you, inspire you, criticize you, and give you structure. My parents did all of these things with their contracts. They tackled every subject. There was nothing we didn't discuss. I didn't love every aspect of it, but I was mature enough to understand that almost everything they talked about made sense." **—DEREK JETER**

DO YOU HAVE WHAT IT TAKES TO BECOME A
JETER'S LEADER?

- I am drug and alcohol free.
- I volunteer in my community.
- I am good to the environment.
- I am a role model for kids.
- I do not use the word "can't."
- I am a role model for my peers and younger kids.
- I stand up for what's right.

- I am respectful to others.
- I encourage others to participate.
- I am open-minded.
- I set my goals high.
- I do well in school.
- I like to exercise and eat well to keep my body strong.
- I am educated on current events.

CREATE A CONTRACT

What are your goals?

Sit down with your parents or an adult mentor to create your own contract to help you take the first step toward achieving your dreams.

For more information on JETER'S LEADERS, visit
TURN2FOUNDATION.ORG

About the Authors

DEREK JETER played Major League Baseball for the New York Yankees for twenty seasons and is a five-time World Series champion. He is a true legend in professional sports and a role model for young people on and off the field and through his work in the community with his Turn 2 Foundation. For more information, visit Turn2Foundation.org.

Derek was born in New Jersey and moved to Kalamazoo, Michigan, when he was four. There he often attended Detroit Tigers games with his family, but the New York Yankees were always his favorite team, and he never stopped dreaming of playing for them.

PAUL MANTELL is the author of more than one hundred books for young readers.